Entwined

Entwined

Zooey J. Miller

Copyright © 2021 Zooey J. Miller.

All rights reserved. No part of this book may be reproduced in any form or by any electronic or mechanical means, including information storage and retrieval systems, without permission in writing from the publisher, except by reviewers, who may quote brief passages in a review.

ISBN: 978-1-63795-742-4 (Paperback Edition)
ISBN: 978-1-63795-743-1 (Hardcover Edition)
ISBN: 978-1-63795-741-7 (E-book Edition)

Some characters and events in this book are fictitious. Any similarity to real persons, living or dead, is coincidental and not intended by the author.

Book Ordering Information

Phone Number: 315 288-7939 ext. 1000 or 347-901-4920
Email: info@globalsummithouse.com
Global Summit House
www.globalsummithouse.com

Printed in the United States of America

Dedicated, in love memory, to my Una for always being there, pushing me to write. And to the friends that have been both inspiring and supportive.

Contents

Home 1
The Gift 9
Prize 14
Obituary 30
Second Chances 37
Bend 54
In Search Of 69
Arrangements 72
Secret Lives 87
Delivery 94
The Exciting Life 102

Home

Life is a test of divine design. Faith is the No. 2 pencil with which we take the test. The Word is the answer book we can reference to pass the test. However, if we lack faith, we cannot take the test, and if we are ignorant of the Word, how can we pass? Yeah, life is a grand Pass or Fail Test. When the Test time is over, we can only hope to read the Word right and our faith-filled in the bubbles correctly. Then the Lamb will call out your name to hand out the reward for making the grade.

~ Street Preacher, Autumn 2000

Taylar closed the worn black and white notebook of recorded quotes and stared at her watch. Kayla was late, and it was far too hot to be outside. Sitting beneath the cloudless bright sky, no matter how beautiful, seemed to worsen the fever, not to mention the sense of anticipation. The train station had emptied, leaving the lonely melodic hum of machinery. Trapped in the lull between trains and transients, Taylar felt out of place, too exotic for the desert population that also called the area home. A mock turtleneck, long banded hair, paint-splattered jeans, and thong sandals were a far cry from the western gear generally seen in those parts. Taylar would have preferred to bypass it and head further west, maybe to the ocean. The bay of San Francisco or the rainy streets of Seattle were more inviting. But Taylar had stopped there, unable to resist the urge to see the desert blossom.

The screeching of tires and the blaring horn brought Taylar out of revelry. The window of the halted Jeep rolled down, revealing the crazed driver behind the wheel. Taylar didn't bother to listen to the apology being yelled out. After tossing the duffel bag into the back, Taylar eased into the passenger seat.

"Still as androgynous as ever, I see," Kayla said. "Are you ever going to decide?" She peeled out of the station.

"Sure, I will, the moment you stop dyeing your hair, Ms. Clairol."

Kayla cast a hard side-eye on her passenger. "Hey, my hair is not up for discussion."

"But my sexuality is always on the docket? Besides, Androgyny is so 80's. Bowie is gone, RIP. Geez, Kayla, you're a psychiatrist; get with the times. The term is nonbinary," Taylar replied coolly.

"I like the term Androgyny. It sounds more organic." Kayla said defensively as she returned her gaze to the road.

Taylar didn't respond; instead concentrated on the cityscape zooming by, effectively shutting down any further talk. The gender debate was an ongoing discussion. Kayla was convinced that Taylar's need to disassociated from gender assignment was a rebellion against a conservative upbringing. Conversely, Taylar would up the ante to say, non-gender assigned was a rebellion against any institution that demanded conformity.

Kayla came to a jerking stop at the next light. That is when she decided to reopen their talk. Taylar could feel her chewing on words in her head, searching for a way to lighten the mood. Usually, she would begin by talking about her work or asking about Taylar's recent escapades. None of those topics began their next conversation.

She cleared her throat and said, "Your parents called me."

She could feel Taylar recoil at the mention of Parents.

The Niancas were not a welcomed topic either. Theirs was not a happy family nucleus due to Taylar's resistance to authority and resentment.

"What did the neurotic alcoholic and fat-ass want?"

Kayla shook her head, exasperated. "Despite their flaws, prodigal child, they are your legal parents. They did provide you a home and support. Therefore, you should give them a call now and again. Scottsdale isn't far. We can drive up there. Just like the old days."

"No, thanks." Taylar's voice was as dry as the air around them.

She let out a deep sigh before continuing, "They adopted again. They want me to be the godmother. And they hope you will come and meet the little girl."

"Poor kid, she should run as soon she can," Taylar replied with much cynicism.

Kayla gave Taylar a disgruntled look. For ten years, she had been listening to Taylar whine about how horrible it was living with the Niancas. Taylar had run away from home more than a dozen times before reaching the age of sixteen. If the state could have had its way,

"Taylar, you're an adult now; you need to address your issues with them."

"I don't have issues with them. I just don't like them."

"They have done a lot for you. Have you conveniently forgotten about all the trouble your truancy and running away caused? "

Taylar would have been sent Juve for truancy, and the Nicanca's jailed and/or fined as well. However, Mr. Nianca had been able to convince Social Services, it was not necessary. He had explained that because Taylar had been adopted at an older age, they were still having some adjustment and growing pains. The judge was agreed and was lenient and assigned them family counseling and some community service actives. However, none of those events had any effect on Taylar. Six months later, the wayward teen wound up in Tucson and bonded to Kayla.

The Memory of their initial meeting drifted across her mind's eye as they entered the suburbs.

* * * *

Kayla had just finished her third year at the Hardaway Institute and was more than ready to celebrate with a quiet meal at home. Coming out of the grocery store, her thoughts were consumed with plans for the future. She was so engrossed with her inner thoughts she stepped off the curb without looking for oncoming traffic. The sound of screeching tires broke her rumination. Kayla's head jerk around, surprised to find a Ford Windstar packed with screaming children had stopped short her and her buggy. Cringing with reprisal offered an apology to the diver, who in turn gave her a disheveled smile and waved her to cross streets. Once safe of range of the through traffic Kay once more entered her trance-like waltz to her car.

This spatial ignorance would lead to the biggest fight of her life.

"Don't move!" A voice commanded her from behind.

Obediently, she remained still, unable to think. A loaf of bread slipped from her fingers into the trunk of the car. Kayla held her eyes together tightly, hearing nothing but a clicking sound. Had she just opened them, she would have seen the camera's flash.

"I wish you hadn't done that." The voice behind her groaned with disappointment. And was three octaves hight than she expected

"The picture came out all wrong." The strange said.

Kayla's eyes popped open, and her brow furrowed. With her hands still in the air, she slowly turned her head to confront her assailant. There Taylar stood, a thin, five foot five package, cursing at the functions on the…weapon. Kayla couldn't believe what she was seeing. The last thing that she intended to find was a teenager holding her hostage…with a camera.

Enraged by the prank, she roared. "What's the matter with you? Get out of here before I call the cops!"

The teen looked from the scowling woman to the Polaroid as if trying to decide which image was more profound. That contemplative look quickly developed into an impish grin.

"Since you've ruined my picture, you have to let me sketch you live." Almond brown eyes stared into Kayla's as a stained chalk hand shoved the Polaroid into a small shirt pocket.

Kayla felt hypnotized by the teen's expression. The warm gaze was so intense that she soon forgot she had been afraid. It didn't take long, though. The clanking and crashing of shopping carts across the parking lot brought her careening back to reality.

This can't be real life. Seriously, Kayla thought to herself.

A random art student wanted her picture. It was too much. It had to be some kind of joke. She analyzed the face before her—long, dark hair, lean form, and a face too pretty for a young man, but an attitude too brash for a young woman. Either way, this person was probably barely legal. Therefore, it had to be a joke. She had planned a quiet evening of dinner with smooth vodka to wash it down, then a nice, warm bath. This kid interrupted her plans.

Kayla steeled herself with a long inhale. Her heart rate was still thundering, but she had to take control of the situation.

As calmly as she could manage, she addressed the strange teen. "It's impolite to sneak up on people. I don't know what kind of game you are playing, but it's dangerous, and you shouldn't do it."

The kid did not move. Instead retorted in a prideful tone, "My name is Taylar Nianca. This is not a game. I'm a serious artist, and I am very *serious* about painting you."

Kayla didn't answer at first. She finished loading her bags into her car, debating with herself about what to do. It was not a normal situation. Now that fear had passed, other thoughts could come to the forefront. Questions floated up first. *Who is the kid? What is its intent? How can I trust this unknown person?* She reevaluated the youth. This time they locked eyes for a few seconds. Something about the kid's eyes captivated her. There was an earnestness in them that put her at ease. But it was her caregiver instincts that pushed the most for her to accept Taylar. As a doctor, her conscience would not allow her to ignore a kid loitering around town. Then again, she could have been in shock. Shock can affect rational thinking. Or she was feeling a little vain. Have a self-portrait was a tempting offer. There was also the feeling that if she refused, she would be missing out on something extraordinary. She took a risk feeling that her instincts were right, and took Taylar home on that hot summer evening. It's a decision she has yet to regret.

* * * *

Coming back to the present, Kayla chuckled to herself. The significant part of that story was she had not been charged with kidnapping. She had used the pretense of wanting a mural painted to get Taylar to stay. She even added a bribe of paying professional rates for the work. The idea of paying gig gave the kid starry eyes. But during that week, she had been placing calls to find out where the little vagrant's real home was. When she had finally contacted Francisco and Betty Nianca, it had taken hours to console them. It took a lot of effort to assure them that she meant Taylar no harm and that she wanted to help reunite. Once they accepted that she was a doctor, they agreed with her plan to reunite their family.

When the Nianacs had come to retrieve Taylar, the young artist was mid stoke on the mural. The kid would have escaped out the backdoor if Kayla had called in a favor from an orderly. The large man had come over early, on the pretense of being in the neighborhood. Taylar was too absorbed in the project to notice the additional presence until it was too late. It had been an intervention type of situation. After a lot of tears, angry words, and ultimatums, a compromise was made. One of the concessions was that Kayla became an unofficial family member and counselor.

And just like Springs of the past, Kayla found herself shuttling a free spirit to her suburban slice of life.

Traffic moved smoothly, allowing them to make it to Kayla's subdivision in record time. For that, Taylar could not have been happier. An early arrival meant escaping a lecture. She parked outside an adobe white home that looked almost like the twenty other homes that lined the street.

Kayla seemed to spring from the Jeep. While Taylar still struggled to pull the duffel the back even as she opened the door.

"Is everything still the same?" Ta

"Yeah, just more cluttered," Kayla replied

Taylar hefted the duffel, "I'm going to open up the attic."

"When do you plan on leaving?" Kayla asked, slinging her bag and keys into a chair in the corner.

Taylar stopped at the bottom of the steps. "When I get my muse back."

A small smirk played across Kayla's lips. "Just remember to lock the door when you leave. You forgot last time."

Taylar just smiled and proceeded up the stairs.

Two weeks passed before they had another semi-normal conversation.

* * * *

Kayla tossed and turned in the heat. Eventually, laying sprawled across the bed, wide awake and sweaty. The ceiling fan whirled overhead, but it was not enough to cool the night's hot air. The clock on the wall displayed two A.M. It gave Kayla a glimmer of hope that deep sleep might come between then and the rise of the sun. Reaching for the glass on her nightstand, she found no refreshment. Kayla groaned, throwing the thin sheet off her legs and pulling her exhausted body out of bed. For some reason, she felt far more tired once on her feet. The house should not be this hot. She vaguely remembered turning on the A/C on the way to bed. Grabbing the empty glass, she exists the bedroom in the hall, she is greeted by the smell of smoke.

"Ugh! Taylar," she growled.

She did not know where the little vagrant picked up the smoking habit. Although Taylar would usually go outside, occasionally, the artist would forget and lit up in the house. In a childish effort to vent the fumes, her guest had turned off the A/C and opened the windows. But, the night breeze was not strong enough to push the smog out. And the heat only made it worse.

The back door of the kitchen was also open, the deck light illuminating the vinyl floor. Kaylar used the cool air of the refrigerator to get relief from the heat. After a moment, she filled her glass from the pitcher on the shelf. She stared at the contents of the fridge, her body rejecting the idea of going back into the sweltering jungle of her bedroom. Reluctantly, she closed the refrigerator and followed the path of light to the patio.

Once outside, she asked, "What's troubling you?"

Taylar's head tilted back into an awkward pose following the sound of the voice.

Pointing a cigarette pointed at the canvas propped between two patio chairs, Taylar asked,

"Who is she?"

Kayla looked over the rim of the glass, pretending to examine the image. She knew what was about to happen. Taylar's version of twenty questions: where was I, what was my inspiration, what year was it, and so on. Unfortunately, she did not have the mental capacity to endure it tonight.

"How should I know?" she replied. "You painted her. You tell me."

The dark head went back up as Kayla sank into the opposite chair.

"I think this was from when I was with that traveling circus," Taylar said. "But I didn't think I kept anything from that tour. Did I even talk about this chick?"

My eyebrow went up. "You talk about a lot of people, especially your patrons."

Kayla could see Taylar's head shaking back and forth. "Whoever she is, she wasn't a patron. A muse, maybe...."

They sat in silence as smoke, and warm air swirled about them. As Taylar's cigarette burned to the end, its ashes fell harmlessly on faded jeans. Kayla dozed off in the chair. Until the scraping of plastic on concrete roused her. Sleepily she watched the painter and canvas disappear into the house. She listened to the sounds of the air conditioner starting up and the clanging of closing windows, but she made no effort to move.

"You should come inside," the artist called to her. "Your bed's more comfortable than a lawn chair. I'm going to go paint."

Kayla sleepily followed the summons, but instead of sleeping in her bed, she dreamed the night away in the attic studio.

The Gift

For Millie Johnson, Wednesday was proving to be more stressful than Monday. Her desk was piled high with proposals, manuscripts, print outs, and literary resources hiding her glorified word processor. Despite all the items demanding her attention, she sat analyzing her e-mail, pondering the order in which to open them. Most of her e-mail was ignorable: corporate memos and messages from clients who had a million questions. The final category was the daily rant from Charlene.

Only one title held her attention:

"FWD. FWD. NEW STAFF. ALL DEPT ORIENTATION."

Millie had a visceral reaction to the words: all department orientation made her cringe. It meant Mr. Funderburke had found someone he wanted to add to the team. But would not place them in one department until he had evaluated their actual value to the company. Funderburke Press was a small Chicago based publisher comprised of an eclectic bunch that supported local writers and authors. Millie had gotten a position as an editor and literary advisor several years ago. At the time, she thought she would pursue journalism while using this position as a stepping stone in that direction. But along the way had settled into the role and let the dream of being a reporter go. It was comfortable, and life was manageable. Although she had to admit that that first year had been miserable. Funderburke insists that everyone understood each other's department before settling into one's final job duties. She was not a fan of the constant change, but she had stuck it out.

Unfortunately, not every new hire was a good fit for the team. More than a few had been unable to handle the orientation process. Some new hires had complained. They postured about not being interns to be bounced around and forced to do grunt work. She found such behavior aggravating. But it also made her respect how Funderburke did things. The job duties could be demanding at times, and one had to soldier through. If the staff could not stand up to the pressure, nothing got put out, and nobody profited. Thomas Funderburke was a visionary with an uncanny knack for recognizing talent. As a result, he had designed a workplace that could quickly weed out the chaff from the grain. Maybe that is why she stayed on so long.

The thoughts of some of her previous trainees still conjured a sour taste in her mouth. But Millie did not want to project her bad experiences onto someone else. So, she scanned the file, looking for insight into the character of Deshawn Clemons. Millie continued to read his bio, looking for clues about his personality and intent. If signing on was just a random decision on Mr. Clemons' part, she didn't want anything to do with him. Millie had worked hard to be "a *credit to the community*," just like Mother wanted her to be. Resulting in zero tolerance for those who did not put a hundred percent into their work. But if this *Deshawn* showed any real interest in the work he might do, she would bend over backward to show him everything she knew.

Still, the entire process just gave her a headache. She would need to dig out the training guides and materials she completed for these instances. The last two new hires to come through her department had been a nightmare. She, as all too happy to see them both go to accounting where they belonged. Millie considered herself an introvert herself, but social skills were not lost on her. To Millie, the finance team was bland and hard to interact with sometimes. Only Charlene got along with them. Then Again, Charlene was a particular case. Her personality was also the reason she had to work with all the new hires.

The editing department has handled a trio comprised of Charlene George, senior editor, the Admin. Assistance Tanya Graves and herself.

Preparing for the inevitable, Millie started making a mental list of the preliminary information she would instill into her new underling. It was the rational thing to do. Not that her job was rocket science, but it had its rules and regulations. Her internal debate was interrupted by the Admin. and delivery man, who was carrying a large parcel that looked as though it had been stamped a thousand times.

"Oh!" The Admin said, coming to a halt right in front of the delivery guy carrying the box.

"Sorry about barging in. I thought you had gone to lunch."

"I have not gone yet. Sir, can lean that again the far wall," Millie replied, pointing to the other side of the room.

Tanya quickly moved aside to let the man complete his task. Once she signed for the package, Millie expected them both to leave her office. However, when the sound of a closing door did not fill the room, Millie looked up from the screen. Tanya was still there, examining the oversized package.

"Aren't you going to open it?" she asked Millie.

"Not yet, Tanya. I have to get through this mountain."

Slowing, Millie brought her attention to the box. She had been expecting anything. And no one she knew would have sent something like to the office. Nor would any of her subscriptions come here. Millie eyed the package, forgetting the whole new hire debacle. For some reason, unexpected delivery didn't sit well with her. Mystery and intrigue were not her forte.

"You never get anything this big," Tanya said.

Pointing a long, manicured fingernail at the writing on the box, Tanya asked, "Is it something you ordered online? I've never heard of TiPiNianca. What do they make?"

Millie got up from her desk to have a better look. Both women stooped in front of the package to read the return address. It had traveled thousands of miles. The sender's name was unfamiliar. Its P.O. Box was even more unknown.

"I have no idea who that is," Millie muttered, moving back to the safe confines of her desk. "Or what this is."

"You're not going to open it? Don't tell me you're not curious. Maybe it's from an admirer?" The look on Tanya's face was reminiscent of a romance-obsessed teen.

Millie raised an eyebrow, looking back at her computer. "I'll wait until I can figure out where it came from."

"Aww, come on, Millie. Where's your sense of adventure?"

Millie gave her a wordless stare that clearly indicated the conversation was over.

Tanya sighed. "Okay, but if you change your mind, I'll gladly help you unwrap it."

Millie was interested in the mystery box. She wanted to finish reading about the training schedule of the newbie.

"I have an idea. Why don't you try looking up the company? Then tell me what you would find. Maybe it belongs to someone else, and we need to return it."

The Admin nodded her head in agreement, "On it!" Tanya happily began her online search for the mystery company. And Millie was glad to have quickly moved this mystery out of her inbox.

Returning to her e-mail once more, She marked her calendar for Deshawn's arrival. She had a few months to prepare for the new arrival. She could just as easily hand him over to Tanya for basic training. But that would not be a good look. And Mr. Funderburke frowned on that sort of thing. Millie closed the calendar with a resigned sigh before moving on to more important correspondence.

Tanya spent the rest of the afternoon fruitless looking for Tipinianca. The return address was just a non-Commercial P.O. box. And to her dismay, Millie still had no interest in opening the parcel.

At five o'clock, Millie was ready to call it a day. She logged off her terminal and retrieved the large tote. For a brief moment, she considered taking some work home, and caved into her need excel and picked up two stacks of bounded papers that needed to be reviewed. Giving the room once last once over for her eyes fell on the package.

An unexpected package is nice, she told herself. B*ut I'd like to know who it came from before* I *open* it. *That way, I know what to expect.*

The TiPiNianca package would have to wait until she had more information on its origin before considering opening it.

Prize

It was supposed to a boring Friday night. Aisha had nothing exciting planned, except a cold beer and neatly rolled joint. That was until the text came in on her secondary phone. It had been idle for days now; it beeped with intent.

The beasts showed up.

A few moments later, two pictures came over. The first image was of a pair of very large white dogs in separate kennels. The second image showed a warehouse beside a low standing parking deck. The meaning of the messages finally connected to Aisha. Bajah was baiting her. She took a long drag from her joint to suppress her annoyance. The place was at the airport. She hated driving in that area because some of the roads were horrible to navigate in the dark.

Months ago, the local hypeman had sent her an invitation to be an exhibitor at his version of the U.S. Dog Show. He had gotten several breeders, groomers, and dog enthusiasts to make this show. She flatly told him no. Aisha did not want it widely known that she was a breeder. Especially considering that she had gotten started under less than aboveboard means. Anyone who came to her came by referral. There was no website, no social media. She used a prepaid phone that she answered once a day. The voice mail was curt and warned that calls would only be returned between 8p and 10pm. Admittedly she was paranoid, but breeding dogs could get dicey. Especially when handling dangerous breeds. She took a lot of precautions when dealing with her clients and Animals.

Looking at the phone again, she frowned. She thought it was a joke when Bajah conceived the idea a year ago. Bajah had come to her kennel to pick up a pair from her litter of Dobermans. Aisha had been watching the U.S. Dog when he arrived. At the time, he had not known about it and had asked her questions. During the event's explanation, she mentioned that the kennel club did not recognize Pitbulls or most established hybrids. Her rant triggered something in her hypeman associate.

With a twinkle in his eyes started planning. Bajah wanted an event that would have the best breeders of the dogs his people liked. Real dogs like bulldogs, pits, Rottweillers, and other mixed mastiff types.

He said, 'I'll call it The Dog Men Kennel Show.' Sis, it'll be dope, and best believe we won't have no 'shit-yous.'

Aisha had given up on correcting his mispronunciation of Shih-Tzu. He was too impressed by his vision to listen.

"It's not the dog that's dangerous, baby girl. It the master ". He said to her as if he had just given her the keys to life.

It was not profound for her. She shared the same sentiment. She put a lot of care into her dogs. Although she had been thrust into the scene, it had become important to her. She could not change the fact there was a possibility that persons with less than humane intents may purchase one of her animals. It was a reality; she accepted when she decided she would take over the business. It had been hard. By the time she got involved, many dogs had to be put down because of illness or ingrained temper. She managed, got the kennel cleaned and quotes filled.

She never would have guessed her beloved dog Max had come from the same place. Her first dog was a mixed breed pit, given to her High School sweetheart Rodney their junior year. Max was a fine dog. And Rodney had raised many other good dogs during the eight years they were together. But what happened after they broke up five years ago, she did not know. The kennel and its dogs were in bad shape. Four years ago, his mother, Mrs. Elly, called saying he had been locked up and she was all alone. And did not know what to do.

Aisha came in and fixed it all. The problem was that some of the buyers were in life. Rodney had been helping them with more than dogs, had gotten caught holding someone's parcel. Getting them to understand she was not going that road had taken more time. But she managed that too, and now she was just used on her project.

She loved hybrids like Max and wanted to breed as many like him as possible. Dear Max died at the ripe old age of 77. Despite his loving and obedient demeanor, he was considered a dangerous breed.

Dangerous that was the keyword in her mind when she thought about Bajah's event. The negative possibilities multiplied in her head. It made her leery about being involved with this event. She didn't know most of these people. Their dogs could be half-trained. The last thing she needed was to be apart of some incident and wind up on the news. That could mess up all her streams of income. Therefore, she had opted out of participating.

She took another puff to calm her thoughts. It was supposed to be a chill Friday night. But the text changed that. The Beasts were in town. She had not gotten anywhere with her own search them. Now, out the blue was Bajah serving them up on a silver platter. Why naysay a gift from the universe.

She was even starting to think they were an urban legend. Granted, she tried to stay out of the shady side of things, but that did not mean she did know things. She had seen pictures. Those dogs were a pair of the most beautiful hybrids she had seen. And she wanted one of them mated to her prize hybrid.

Imagining the litter made her giddy. She ran different scenarios in her head of how the pups would look. Considered did training methods. And of course, calculated the possible profits. She considered keeping the 1st litter all to herself. Raising them to test their temperament. Or selling one or two to vetted people to compare the animal's behavior and trait.

Aisha took her project very seriously. She cared about three things, Mrs. Elly, her dogs, and her money. Anything or anyone that interfered with her having that tetrarchy was not tolerated.

As she looked out the kitchen window, she could see the outline of the kennel. The dogs were quiet. She may have a few more than the city ordinance allowed. But the neighborhoods did not complain. At her feet her a newly acquired two-year-old pharoh was sleeping. She had named him Shel. She took a pull from her joint looked at the phone again. It *might be worth it to go*, she thought.

Still dressed in her business clothes, a white shirt and black pencil skirt, all she had to do was put on her shoes and go. She could take the dog, too; Shell needed some socializing. She could drive forty minutes to talk to this dude about his dogs, and things could work out.

Otherwise, she could do all that, and things wouldn't work out, and she'd have wasted half a tank of gas and blown her high. She took another pull before snuffing out the bud.

"Shell," she said, waking the little red hound.

"We're going out."

The hound tilted his head but did not move until she grabbed the keys and his leash.

* * * *

The venue was not typical, but neither was the event. She didn't know how many sponsored he coaxed into handing over their hard-earned money to support this event, but the people had come. The parking lot was a buzz. It was past midnight, and people were still pulling into the deck behind her. Some had their dogs like her. While others were spectators.

Out of the car and approaching the building, Aisha noted the security. She paid the cover fee and entered. And was met with a row of vendor booths. There were groomers and homemade food producers, breeders, and everything else you could want for your dog. Aisha nodded her head at sight, approvingly. It was like a midnight pop up shop for dogs. But she knew more than as happens, so she proceeded down the hall.

Along the way, she saw some familiar faces of the people. Some she made an effort to greet others, she stirred clear.

As she approached what looked like another entry, there was another round of security. The bleeping wand check made her giggle. It was like going to the airport. Ironic since they were only a mile from it. For all, she knew these guys could be TSA on a side hustle. After getting the green light, she proceeded into a larger open area. Through the door, pockets of people gathered.

But she was only looking for one person among them. Several times she was stopped by people asking her about her little hound. The oddity of her little rabbit hunting dog garnered more attention than she thought. But it was good the dog needed to be socialized. Although he tended to cower behind her knees, he accepted the strangers' attention, which made her very proud.

Overall, she liked the setup. There set up rings across the floor space where handlers were showing off their dogs. From her vantage, she could tell that different tracks held different types of dogs. Behind the ring sat a judge and some enforcer type to ensure that some of these less behaved dogs stayed in line.

Aisha could tell from sight that some of the dogs were not regular house pets. Some of them had seen scrapes. Good, that Bajah had had the foresight to have people on the floor who could take action should the dogs attack each other or people.

She pressed deeper into the structure. She got the sense that a lot of money was moving about the room. The seen dollar was obvious, the admission, the liquor, the vendors. The cash prizes, but she wondered about what she was missing.

She came upon a roped-off section of the facility. It may have been an open office space or some other closed series of rooms at one point. The door to that area swung open briefly as scantily clad server exited. There was some of the side money she had been wondering about. At a glance, she could see a dice table and free-flowing bills.

That room did not concern her, and she continued. Her thoughts shifted back to the white beasts. Looking back over the rings, she did not see anything that matched the photos she had. In the picture, she saw the kennels where the dogs were kept. But now that she had arrived, she couldn't tell they could be.

It had heard from a source that the owner didn't like for anybody to be near his animals. *And this was as public as one could get. Where could someone like that be?*

Her thoughts were interrupted by the event announcer. They had live entertainment coming to the stage. Aisha admonished herself for noticing. She was caught up in her mission. She looked out at the floor again and realized that some of the rings were being broken down. Panic started to set in.

Did *I miss them? Did I spend too much time procrastinating?*\She h paused by stage to evaluate the situation.

A crowd had gathered and was cheering for the rapper. Aisha did not recognize the song but liked his stage, *The Golden Child*. When she would busy, she decided to add him to her playlist. But right now, she more important things to do than pretend to be a fan.

As she cleared the stage area, she noticed Bajah heading her way.

The host sauntered about the rings, greeting his guests. Everyone there knew that golden smile. That evening, he was escorted by two big Doberman bitches, acquisitions from a seller he couldn't wait to see.

"Aisha! Baby girl, long time, no see!" As the host approached his guest, the hound hid behind her mistress's leg. The host leaned in close to embrace an old friend.

He had seen her come in earlier, looking like she was ready for a power lunch and not a party with the dog men. He respected her all-business demeanor. It was why he gave her a tip. Knew that was what brought her out tonight,

"Where are they?" she looked around the crowd.

He shifted, pulling his dogs from the little hound.

"See the green curtain in the corner and the guy in the chair."

She looked in the direction, he indicated, "Yeah."

"Tell the guy I sent you."

Aisha rolled her eyes. She did not like cloak and dagger games. But she would play along.

As she made her way in that direction, she could tell the guy was sizing her up. She could hear some sounds she did not want to hear beneath the beats of *The Golden Child*.

Beside her, she could feel the puppy's apprehension. Didn't want to be there.

Aisha paused to console him. "Trust your mama." "Places like this build character."

She gave the man the password, and he drew back the curtain.

"They are on the far wall," he said quickly and let the tarp drop in place. The scene was more of what Aisha had expected to see. This building must have been in the process of being converting to a gym with a pool. The large open floor and glass front rooms along the back made more sense. The area she had come to was going to be the pool. But now that would pool was being used as a fighting pit.

She ignored everything but the two isolated, locked, and chained kennels. She had a feeling this was going on. Granted, it was way low key, but she still didn't want to know. Looking around to orientate herself, she caught the eye of a handler she had dealt with in the early days. He had given some good advice. They shared a non-verbal greeting, and she continued her search.

Finally, she spotted the dogs. Strange, they seemed to be alone. Rumor had it that the owner of that pair shot anyone who came within six feet of his dogs. It was a good thing that security was on site. Although anyone with violent intentions didn't need a gun to make their point, a broken bottle worked just as well. Aisha continued forward with resolve.

The bull match ended in a short and rough victory. Full of energy, the M.C. rushed to begin the next match, hyping up the crowd with promises of a good brawl.

She patted his copper flanks, and they moved deeper into danger. At seven feet from the kennel, Aisha could make out two snow-white dogs. At six feet, the albinos started barking. One dog circled in his cage as if to gain momentum to launch an attack. The other crouched and snarled.

At five feet, Aisha knew she was in trouble feeling a sharp poke in her side. The pup whimpered and started shaking, expelling the contents of his bladder.

"What do you want?" The bass of that threatening voice excited Aisha more than she wanted to admit. A mischievous smile shaped her lips.

She could tell her attacker was a tall man. The rumors were true; he did not like anyone near his dogs. *The calmest way to defuse the situation is to stand perfectly still.* Aisha told herself.

It worked to calm most beasts. Sometimes the same technique worked on people. At that moment, she had few choices. She had no allies there, no protection, yet, she was excited. Aisha's exhilaration ran deeper than the pride of watching one of her whelps win its first match.

Adrenaline spread through her veins.

I don't miss this kind of high, she said to herself, *but I need one of those dogs. I wish I hadn't smoked that joint.*

She tried to think clearly, but her senses were out of control, her vision blurred by the fluorescent lights. The chanting from the next fight rang in her ears. Her tongue was dry as sand, and the scent of her assailant filled her nostrils. The combined sensations only succeeded in making the glass pressed against her side feel painfully satisfying, resulting in her reckless reaction of leaning into the makeshift weapon. She was sure he would pull it back. He was just bluffing to test her nerve. But if he didn't back down, that glass was going to slide right into her chocolate-truffle skin.

"Step off, broad." The attacker tightened his grip and pressed a little harder, solidifying his promise.

But Aisha stood fast. Her tetanus was up to date, and, besides, she had two to five minutes to get help before she suffocated from the punctured lung.

"I have a bitch I wanted to be mated," she said as calmly as possible.

As he shifted, she felt his eyes examining her and the puppy. "Leave."

He took some of the pressure off his weapon, indicating she should escape. Instead, she stood there, wavering between staying and leaving. She decided to stay.

She decided to play her river card. "Baja's Dobermans came from my kennel. He told me you bred that pair special. I can tell they aren't Cane Carso. The one I have at home is special." She pulled out her phone, letting hold on her dogs' leash slide her elbow. She had to let the pup know she was in control. He was still whining and shaking at her side. She was glad she had not brought Doris. The attacker would likely be missing some calve muscle by now. But Shell was still a puppy and soft.

She held the phone at an angle to give him a view of her prize mix.

There was a pause before he answered. "You the one he's been going on about?"

"Depends. What'd Bajah say?" Aisha asked with a tone too playful for her current situation.

"He says he knows a broad who breeds dogs and is very interested in hybrids."

"Then I would be the one."

He gave her more space. She used the opportunity to turn and get a look at her prospective partner. He was definitely an eye full, a very handsome eye full.

"If you're done here, I can take you to examine her, and we can talk terms."

He sized her again, his long locs swaying with the tilt of is his head. His eyes landed on the little red hound at her side. Aisha was slowly becoming jealous of the attention her animal was receiving.

"He was a gift," she stated defensively.

The man knelt to get a closer look at the cowering dog, his eyes dark and intense.

"This one looks well cared for. I'll see your Dam."

Aisha smile smugly. Her level of jealousy simmered to low.

"If you are done here, we can go now."

He stood to his full height and encroaching on her space. His proximity allowed Aisha to appreciate his features and scent. He was trying to intimidate her again. The action made her smile broaden. She was too excited and high to cowed.

"Eager?" he seemed to growl in her ear.

"Patience is not my virtue. Now or never," Aisha retorted.

He backed off, returning her smile, "meet me at the gas station at the top of the street in thirty minutes."

Aisha nodded, scooping up the neglected leash and, sauntered away. She wanted to do a cartwheel but held in her enthusiasm.

Turning abruptly mid-sashay, Hey, what do I call you. ?

"Ulysses."

The next chain of events happened in a smooth sequence. They met at a determined time and location. The drive from the Southside to the northeast seemed to take less time than usual. The hound stuck his head out the passenger window, grinning at the world as they floated by. Avoiding checkpoints, the Caddy left the skyline in the distance, exchanging it for the suburbia's darkness. Aisha checked her rearview mirror to make sure that she was being followed. She felt as giddy as a mad scientist. It had taken a long time to track those dogs, longer than she had expected. The rumors had not done them justice. Now just had to convince the owner to sign on.

She guided them into a neighborhood where the trees were old and towering. Their branches were heavy with leaves rustled in the summer breeze. At that hour, all the houses were dark. No one would take notice of the late-night transgression. Aisha had to swallow a drop of shame that swelled up inside her as she flipped on her turn signal. *Soon*, she thought, *this place will go back to being just a house*. Turning into a gravel driveway of an older ranch style home.

There was a tall privacy fence that wrapped the property. The Caddy came to a stop at the edge of the fence. And with a push of a button, the gate rolled back. When the van has come to a stop behind her. Aisha left the car with the puppy following close behind. Sober in the night air, she signaled her guest pull into the back yard.

The van rolled forward until she signaled him to stop. Once parked, the prospective partner exited the vehicle. When he was close enough, she turned on the lights of her half-submerged compound. As they entered the post and wire kennel, some of the dogs began growling. Aisha said 'Down,' sternly, eying each one. The animal instantly stopped.

"These are my breeding pairs. They have been through training. I don't tolerate dogs that can't be trained." She began explaining. Hoping to impress her guest

"What do you do with the unruly ones?" Ulysses asked while eyeing his surroundings.

The back yard was modest, and the kennel set up, and large shed took up most of the area.

"They are culled or sold to certain buyers." She said flatly

"Harsh," He said, taken aback.

"Yes. I do it as humanely as possible. But their life is my responsibility. I cannot allow them to become threats." Despite the conviction in her voice, her face conveyed disappointment and sadness. She was not what he had expected.

He did not say anything else, Aisha continued.

"My dames and studs are well cared for. I have a strict breeding rotation. The Dobermans and Pits. When the puppies are weaned, I take them to start training."

"Where ?"

"Outside of the city. Like children, they need room to run and grow. The neighbors appreciate it. And I don't draw unwanted attention. This little hound is my dog and is still being trained. The one you are about to meet will be my queen." She trailed off as they approached the last kennel.

"Sit, Shell," the hound eased onto his hunches when told. Aisha stopped in front of an inhabited cage and let out a low whistle. A blue-gray bitch trotted forward. The animal's face seemed to curl into a smile as the woman kneeled to give affection. The bonding moment was cut short as she rose to walk the dog forward to greet the stranger. Shell whined in jealousy at her heels.

"You were probably skeptical when you saw me with the red hound. Shell was a trade. But this girl right here is my prize. Her name is Doris."

She motioned from him to come forward and to inspect the dog. Slowly he lowered his hand to allow a sniff test. The dog inhaled then snorted before lowering her head. His hands quietly felt the dog's frame. Judging by his facial express Aisha was assured that he appreciative of her dog's powerful form.

"Seems powerful, I'll give you that," he said, continuing to feel the dog's muscles.

"This coat is a unique color and texture, a short course blue. You don't see that every day. This head is huge and wrinkled. Some kind of Molossoid type? How many breeds did you mix?"

He stepped back for another overall look.

"Three," she said. "The progenitor, Max, was already mixed: pit and Shar-Pei. He was this color. I mated him with a grey Cane Carso. Then, I kept a female from the first litter and mated her with a lilac Shar-Pei. I contracted to have another litter with Max and Grey Cane Carso. Then I had an idea, mate one from Max's second litter and one from Ophelia's first litter. I've been lucky. There have been no muscular-skeletal defects.

He gave an affirming snort. Then look around the kennel again. As if searching for the dogs Aisha mentioned earlier.

"I don't keep all my dogs here—only the ones I plan to breed or are ready to pup. I don't run a puppy mill, Sir. Those Dobermans at the front are courting, so when she ready, the process doesn't have to be forced. The pregnant female in the corner is Ophelia. I have buyers for all her pups. That will be her last litter. I will spay her and find her a nice home to good when the pups are sold. Doris, here will replace her as my breeder. My dogs are strong, smart, and loyal."

"How do you pay for this setup?" he questioned, looking at her spread.

"Cash, of course. But I will take trade occasionally. The red hound sitting so patiently was traded for a Doberman. A whim." She knew that wasn't the answer he was looking for.

She kept her attention on Doris. Using a tied on a bandana to wipe up some of the drool.

"If you decide to stud me one of your males, I want to mate him with Doris. Unless she decides to tuck tail."

The guy scoffed, crossing his arms. "Lady, you are a bundle of contradictions. What are you trying to breed, Frankenstein? She's hardly aggressive. This beast is just an oversized mutt. "

Aisha gasped, genuinely offended by his comment.

"Mutt!? Are you kidding me?! Doris is a beautiful hybrid, the perfect example of strength and obedience. Yes, having a third breed in her bloodline increases the risks of genetic defects and other abnormalities. I have done my homework. It's why I have my dogs thoroughly tested before choosing my breeding pairs to ensure the pups the highest quality."

Aisha had begun petting the animal again subconsciously, admiring her creation and calming her nerves.

"I heard that your dogs are exceptional from some people and hoped you might be willing to share. You've been billing them as Cane Carso, and I can tell they are not from a glance. There is Drogo in their blood, or my name isn't Aisha."

He waved his hand dismissively. "Your experiments don't interest me."

Aisha stared the. "Then why did you come. A litter from this pair could create a new breed for home or ring. Your fighters look like hybrids to me. So how can you look down your nose at mine."

Her guest paused before asking, "Is there anyone else involved in this project?"

She rolled her eyes and pursed her lips. "No one that would interest you."

He stroked his goatee, still thinking. "You keep records on this mutt?"

Without a word, Aisha locked her treasure away again and led her guest out of the kennel. She gestured for him to follow her into the adjoining shed. They followed a footpath lit by small solar lights to the shed. Aisha opened the door and turned on the light in the blink of an eye.

She pulled a photo album from a built-in shelf as he sank into the chair on the other side of the desk.

"This is Dori's files. Her shots medical record and lineage information. She'll be ready to mate in two months. I do request your male be muzzled. The pin with the Dobermans will be there. "Aisha explained, handing over a sizable notebook.

This she was in the crucible of her pitch she was starting to notice something seemed off. She never had to go through this much effort. She had a good rep. Her dogs were good. She was discreet. That was always good enough. And the why he was pouring over the records of Doris seemed a little too exacting.

"I coming here may be an inconvenience to you, but I can afford you a decent place to stay and the Fee to stud. That should be reasonable compensation.

Wearily she leaned against the door jam. The security light for the back of the house was shining in, flooding the room with more light allowing her to observe this prospect more closely.

"I not keen on this idea. My dogs are likely to tear her apart even with the muzzle. I think you miscalculated." He commenting, looking up from the pages.

She gave him a level stare. "How much do you want for a stud?"

He gave her a dispassionate snort. "How many others have you approached? You give them the same offer, or am I special?"

Perhaps her high was wearing off now. Or maybe it was the way this man was trying not to be obvious about memorizing the things in her office. But the danger lights in her head were starting to flash bright red.

"My other business associates have nothing to do with the discussion. I'll admit I've been a fan of your dogs, but if you don't want to … or can't stud them, you could have said so."

Leaning back in the chair. "I only came because I was curious. I'm not into breeding guard dogs. Is that what this really about. Breeding designer guard dogs for wanna be kingpins?"

She was getting angrier by the minute. The flashing red light in her mind pulsed faster. There was a metallic gleam coming from the shelf on her left-hand side, just out of reach. She could have smack herself. She had meant to move that pistol to under desk weeks ago. *Dammit! who is this guy?* I don't want to have to shoot someone tonight.

Her mental red light was flashing a mile a minute.

She had been too excited about the call, too hyped that her project was near completion. She had missed the signs. That civil servant thought he would get her to snitch, or worse, pin her with something.

Note to self, she thought, *the feds are now employing very attractive, smooth-talking, Micah Phifer look-a-likes.*

"I can't help but wonder…" he was said, running his finger around in a circle on her desk. "How did a corporate girl like you get involved with the likes of Bajah?"

"I have no time for games," she snapped. "Either you're in, or you're out."

The mole stood up from Aisha's chair. "I was hoping you would convince me that your cause was worth my time."

Aisha folded her arms. Eyeing harshly. *Am I paranoid? He is trying to flirt? Naw! These guys are way more direct.* It was clear, the negotiations were over.

"See you around," he said smoothly, rising from his seat.

Leaning over the desk, he slipped a card into the waistband of her skirt before exiting the shed.

When she heard the van startup, she vented her anger on her desk. Not that the solid punch did much damage, but what else could she do? She couldn't blame anyone but herself. She was on Fed Radar and hitting one of their agents was a bad idea. Trouble had come her way with a capital T. That meant a big headache.

She whipped out her secondary cell and sent a text to her silent partner. The old man hardly slept, so she was sure he would see it. Mr. Dawkins was a cantankerous old man. However, they had managed an accord built on mutual needs.

He was facing his farm's foreclosure. Aisha wanted to build a Kennel and pet boarding house. His land was the perfect site. And they worked it out that Aisha paid for his back taxes and liens. In return, Mr. Dawkins stayed on the land, took care of the dogs, and oversaw the new building's construction.

At first, Mr. Dawkins was reluctant. They had had several phone calls and visits detailing her plans for the land. Once she explained her end game, he was more amiable. Moving all her dogs to the Mint Hill Farm had always been a part of her end game. The old man kept his farm, and her dogs had a 5-acre dog run and a renovated barn as a kennel—a win-win. The Barn was nearly complete. Doris and Shell would remain with her in the house. She did not like having to be so far from dogs. But do what she had in mind it was necessary.

Mr. Dawkins, you may have unwelcome guests. Just show them the envelope I gave you.

That was all she sent. But was certain the old man would understand. They had had conversations about worst-case scenarios. She also sent a text to Bajah.

I don't like him.

Obituary

Deshawn paced his apartment. The powers that be had decided that it should rain on his day off. He had just finished his first week in the editing department. It had gone fairly smooth. Once the weekend arrived, he found himself trapped inside. Regretfully he had nothing to distract him from the gloom he was feeling.

A memorial day was fast approaching, and the weather certainly set the mood. Among the books on Deshawn's shelves, there is a photo album. The album is half empty. It contains a collection of images for younger days. He opens it with ceremonial propriety. Flipping through the plastic-covered photos, he smiles at some of the memories. He shakes his head at others, remembering those wistful days. The faces on the images toward the end repeat more often. Those pictures are of him and his best friend. There are images of them at school, at home, or out have fun—the contents of the album shrink after their graduation photos. The final two pages contain a newspaper clipping and notebook paper penned in his hand. Solemnly he read his melancholy rendition of his best friend's death.

> "Watcher did not see him die.
> It doesn't matter,
> Dead men are irrelevant.
> Watcher observes a corpse.
> Roll away limp form

Shrug it off, and forget it
In an avenue, she slumps, Witnesses granny's theft.
Behind you, another victim.
Battered and violated
All this in the rain
Tread home to suburbia
Stand before your door, Watcher.
Do you hear the storm?
Thunderclaps hide ill intent.
His keys in hand, coughing blood.
Officer, your perp
Has blended into the night.
So sad, mistaken Watcher.
Irrelevant, boy
Shot down in the dead of night."

Every Autumn, Deshawn read that passage to himself as a reminder that he was living for two. They had been hopeful and optimistic about their futures. They had plans. They were not going to be anyone's statistic. However, tragedy and injustice happened. Deshawn vowed to do all things they both wanted to do.

* * * *

"I'm sorry, Mom. I can't make it to Mr. Gibson's funeral." Holding the phone away from her ear, Aisha half-heartedly listened to her mother whine about how ungrateful and self-centered attitude.

"Aisha, you owe that man," the woman on the other end said, still lamenting that she had raised such an ungrateful child.

Aisha's mother failed to realize that her youngest child hated the very idea of funerals.

What was she to do? Stand there and cry as she watched his body being lowered into the ground? Mr. Gibson would love that, she thought.

Aisha could hear his voice as clearly as if he were standing right next to her. "Aisha, stop ogling. Don't you have better things to do? You'll have enough time to laze about when you're dead!"

Despite her mother's ranting, Aisha knew she respected the man. She owed him her life and career. Mr. Gibson was the father she wished for.

She remembered meeting her so-called real father when she was very young. She hadn't thought much of him and was grateful he stayed away. She had her mom and the aunts. What did she and her brother need with a father? Or any other male figure?

That was until she hit puberty and lost her mind. Her older brother, Jeffery, had gotten a scholarship to an out of state college and was gone just as she was entering high school. Unlike her brother, she hated school. She preferred to follow her cousin Patches in and out of trouble. Or duck out on school to go boost at the mall and chill around the way. The spring Aisha turned fifteen, she found herself facing community service or juvenile hall. That was when, out of nowhere, her Aunt Tina brought Mr. Gibson to the hearing. He said a few words on behalf of the family. He offered his tax and financial services office as the site of her community service.

The word funeral brought Aisha back to the present, but her mind quickly ducked back into her memories.

Come to think of it, Mr. Gibson hadn't even gone to his son's funeral. What was the kid's name? I think it was Jason.

The old goat had said, "What can I do for a dead boy?"

Aisha had snooped through his papers and found out that the son was from a failed marriage. The ex-wife wanted to be as far away as Gibson's money could get her. Gibson thought he was doing the right thing by staying away. There would be no reconnecting for him and his son; a few years later, the kid had been killed shortly after his high school graduation. The shooter was a local authority and never brought to justice. Jason Gibson had been miss identified as a burglar.

Under his workaholic exterior, however, Gibson was torn up about it. Aisha supposed that his regret was her good fortune. He showed her the tricks of his trade to the letter and made sure she was a chartered accountant before graduating from high school. He even convinced her to get an associate degree. Aisha owed Gibson for teaching her how to be independent. The guilt started to set in.

"Alright, Mama," she finally said. "I'll go to the wake."

* * * *

Tanya's mentor, Beatriz Dixon, had left this world. Her father called her to tell her about the funeral. It seemed unreal to Tanya. How could Mrs. Beatriz die? Mrs. Beatriz had been her mentor. But, as it often happened with mentors and students, the student grew up and went away. Mrs. Beatriz became the person Tanya called on holidays and special occasions. A funeral would qualify as a special occasion. Tanya decided that she would ask for time off to fly down to North Carolina and pay her respects.

It wouldn't be until she arrived at the church that Tanya would realize how hard Mrs. Beatriz's passing would hit her.

Tanya returned to her hometown as quiet as a ghost. She stayed in her father's house, only to have him give her a disappointed look because she could only stay for two days. He explained that she would have to give his condolences to the family because he had to pick more hours at the plant. Tanya had already known she would have to do that, even without him asking. Her Old Man wasn't going. He didn't handle death well. His way of coping was to work more hours at the plant. As a little girl, dear old dad had gone to work and made sure he could pay the bills and bury her mother. But otherwise, he wasn't available. Thankfully, Ms. Beatriz had stepped in and helped to raise Tanya into womanhood.

The familiar roads weren't as familiar as they should have been. Tanya almost lost her way to Mt. Zion A.M.E. She entered the church quietly, respectfully, and composed. At least until she saw that cold head. In an instant, she was inconsolable. Mrs. Beatriz had been Tanya's North Star. Who knew it would be so heart-wrenching not to be able to say thank you?

"Why are you gone?" Despite the stares and murmurs. Tanya had given up her seat in the back pew to weep in front of a mahogany casket. "You're always supposed to be here!"

Funerals were supposed to be quiet memorials for the dead. But somehow, a bereaved tramp had found her way into their somber gathering, and she wailed more than the entire family. The ushers knew it would be best to let her cry and say goodbye. But that did not stop the old women from disapproving sentiments about Tanya's outfit.

"Let the young woman be," one of the old women whispered. "She ain't hurting a soul."

The pastor continued his sermon, hoping his words of the blissful afterlife that had embraced their church mother would give the mourners comfort. That was what they had hoped for when the next tearful sobs erupted from Tanya.

The congregation began to sing, "*Swing Low, Sweet Chariot,*" and the pallbearers were approaching. Tanya had not let go of Beatriz's cold fingers.

Before the bearers had to pull her away, someone called out to her. "Tanya?"

The voice that called her was familiar. The vote was comforting and beguiling that it nearly brought her out of her grief.

Tanya vaguely remembered the round laugh-lined face before her. The woman had the kind of look Tanya hoped she would have in old age; smooth, brown, and slightly lined. The matron's light brown eyes shone with wisdom and understanding; she even smiled. It was the kind of smile people gave to those in mourning, the one where they are about to say something you may not want to hear.

"Tanya, it's time to let go," one of the matrons called.

But that smile didn't make Tanya feel worse. Maybe it was because that kind soul offered her a sincere measure of concern and sympathy. Gently, the woman pulled Tanya's fingers into her own hands and guided her away to the pews. Tanya's tears subsided for a moment. Now that her vision was a little clearer, she could think about who she was sitting with. The shock only added to her fatigue.

It was Ms. Elly. Her father had called months before and said that Ms. Elly had to be put in the nursing home because she had lost her faculties. Contrary to that, there, Ms. Elly sat as alert and vivacious as ever.

Then the casket was closed and hefted, initiating another flood of tears. Ms. Elly gave her a handkerchief. Studying the girl's sorrow, she waited for a pause between sobs to speak.

"Bea talked about you the most," she said. "She worried about you a lot, her little lamb. She said you were too sensitive to things around you."

"She's dead." It was all Tanya could get out.

"Only her earthly body is dead. Bea's soul has gone on to the Lord."

Tanya remained quiet as the church mother continued. "Bea spent her life doing what she was called to do. To work with you, young people. It was her calling. A lot of y'all turned out fine. Some were just taken by the devil."

"She was the original life coach," Tanya finally said. "A real positive influence. Kept me grounded, taught me to be a lady. All that stuff they talk about in after-school specials. There aren't too many like Mrs. Beatriz out there anymore."

"Why don't you take up her yoke? Continue her good works. It might do you and someone else some good." Ms, Elly suggested.

Feeling like she had heard the voice of the Holy Spirit, Tanya gaped at the woman holding her hands. Until that very instant, she felt as though she had been on the right track. One simple suggestion shifted and remolded everything she had thought was supposed to make her complete.

She hugged Ms. Elly and said what she had been unable to speak to Beatriz Dixon. "Thank you."

* * * *

"Good morning, Tanya," the person approaching Tanya's desk said.

"Good morning, Ms. George. Here are your messages."

Tanya appeared to be oddly rejuvenated. Just two days ago, she had pleaded for the day off. Tanya's boss marveled at her and wondered if she had been hoaxed.

"I thought somebody had died, the way you carried on the other day," Charlene George said as she flipped through the papers in her hand. "Are you sure you are all right?"

Tanya was hoping that she could avoid talking about what happened with her tactless boss. At least Millie had the decency to respect her privacy.

"My Godmother died," she replied flatly.

"You have my condolences." They were empty words. Sometimes Charlene spoke without empathy. They ... What's this?" Charlene pulled a pamphlet out of her stack. It was from the local youth mentoring agency.

"Sorry. That's mine." Tanya hastily reached over to retrieve it.

A penciled eyebrow went up.

"It's amazing," Charlene said. "Amazing how the dead can inspire the living."

Tanya sat there, quietly fuming at that callous woman. It was too early in the morning for banter. Thankfully, Deshawn appeared at just the right moment, saving her from the editor's cynical commentary on life and death.

"Hello there, you must be Charlene. I am Deshawn Clemons, the new guy, its nice to finally meet you," he said, extending his hand.

"Humph. The new apprentice. Tanya, I'll be in my office for the rest of the day." Charlene George sauntered away, humming some Disney song, without shaking his hand.

"That was pleasant," sarcasm lacing his tone.

"She acknowledged you, so it's a good start," Tanya said cheerfully.

Deshawn gave an inquisitive look. "Care to explain?"

Tanya was reorganizing her cluttered desk. ". Millie says it's best to ignore anything she says that isn't work-related."

Deshawn sneered. "With an attitude like that, it must be hard."

Tanya shrugged. "She's brilliant and tolerable when it comes to working. It's only difficult when Charlene decides to be social. Mr. Funderburke is one person she seems normal around. He's the only man I've seen her willingly talk to. So, continue to stay clear."

Deshawn let out a deep breath. "Just when I was beginning to think it would be okay to work in an office full of females."

Second Chances

"Let me die. Let me die," the woman whimpered from her bed as nurses and orderlies converged on her.

The orderlies had to drag her from the bathroom and hoist her onto the bed. One checked her vital signs, while others struggled to get the stomach pump down her throat.

The woman hurt, hurt everywhere, body, mind, and soul, all at once. She was ready to let go. She was prepared for the hurting to stop. Living just hurt too damn much. It was her memories of what she had gained that were the source of her sadness. Her American dream would not fade away. There was Nothing that would make the emptiness inside her go away. Trying to move on only seemed to make the pain worse, and the world was more frightening because of her fear of pain. Living in fear was just as bad as living in sorrow. She was a woman who had lost everything.

There was only one thing left to dispose of: her life.

"Mrs. Brighton? Mrs. Brighton, can you hear me?" The Doctor flashed his penlight at her dilated irises.

Despite all the anguish, she thought she had already endured, her body seemed to want to endure a little more. She heard the call of the man trying to pull her back from death.

* * * *

"Harris, are you sure you want to take this patient on?" Frustration filled the chief psychologist's voice. "Mrs. Brighton has been here for years, most of that time on suicide watch. She had proven to be an obstinate and unresponsive patient."

"I am well aware of that, Dr. Stephens," the new resident at Hardaway Institute said. "I've been through her file several times. I think if we change our approach, we may be able to make some progress."

Dr. Kayla Harris was rather young for the profession, but she came with outstanding accolades from former professors and employers. Hardaway needed "fresh blood," as the administrators put it, but what they really needed was more funding. The only way to get it was to show that Hardaway was a progressive and lucrative institution, not just a nursing home for the mentally unstable. The administration had thus decided to update the institution's treatment methodology. Many believed that personal attention would be the new prevailing wind in treatment. But Stephens was old school.

He believed in the power of pharmacology and was leery of this so-called New Age medicine. Kayla was New Age from the way she walked and talked to her *Clairol* red locks. Stephens disliked her on sight. He decided he would test the new resident by letting her have one pet project in addition to her regular patients. This pet project would be treated with the new methodology. And would have to show a substantial change in time for Harris's one year review. Mrs. Brighton was the last patient he expected her to choose.

Kayla had chosen Alice Brighton for one simple reason: her method was designed for that type of patient, for the ones that were hiding from the world.

"All right, Dr. Harris," said Dr. Stephens with a sigh. "You can begin your sessions with the patients tomorrow. Good luck."

* * * *

Mrs. Brighton was sitting in her darkroom, listening to the sounds of the morning. According to Mrs. Brighton, everything started at dawn. She was mildly surprised to hear a tap at her door. It was still early for rounds to begin. She didn't move. Whoever it was would enter, no matter what she said.

"Good morning, Mrs. Brighton," An unfamiliar voice chirped. "Can I come in? The floor nurses said you're usually awake at this hour. The sunrise must be lovely."

The unfamiliar Doctor made her way to the windows. "Let me open the blinds for you. It's a beautiful morning."

Mrs. Brighton's voice was curt and sharp. "Don't open them!"

The Doctor paused in front of the window. "All right. May I at least turn on the light?"

Mrs. Brighton waved her hand at the Doctor. "If you must." The Doctor flicked the light switch, filling the room with the soft artificial glow of fluorescents. "I am Dr. Kayla Harris. You can call me Kayla."

The resident arched her eyebrow.

"Humph," she said. "You are woefully young for that title."

"Do you want breakfast?" Kayla asked, ignoring Mrs. Brighton's insult.

"What breakfast? The kitchen isn't open yet."

Kayla shrugged. "All I know is that there's food downstairs. If you want it, Alice."

"Toast and coffee will be fine."

Kayla feigned shock. "That's it? They have real food. I mean, like bacon and eggs kind of food."

Mrs. Brighton wasn't taking the bait. "It's too early for all that."

"Okay, then, when I come back, we'll have a chat." She walked from the room, closing the door behind her.

As Kayla passed the nurses' station, a group of nurses stopped her.

"Well?" they asked her. "Tell us what happened."

"Nothing happened. Excuse me. I'm going to get Mrs. Brighton and myself some breakfast." As she walked to the elevator, she could still hear them talking.

"Oh boy," exclaimed one nurse, "does she have her work cut out for her with that one."

"Yeah," said another nurse. "I heard her kids put her in here and haven't seen her since."

"Yeah, Brighton's mean alright," said a third. "You're lucky you haven't seen one of her episodes."

Hoping to glean some useful information about the patient, Kayla paid close attention to what those chatterboxes were saying. She had studied the notes in Mrs. Brighton's chart, but the notes were only clinical observations. Those renditions were generic and lacked the insight of candid personal opinion. Committing the nurse's conversation to memory, the Doctor could wait to find out how much it turned out to be factual or just plain gossip. At best, she might even witness some of the patient's habits that very morning.

When Kayla returned, Mrs. Brighton was sitting in her rocker, humming, and staring at the blank wall. Setting the breakfast tray on a serving table, the Doctor leaned against the far wall to look around the room. She was hoping to find a clue into what made Alice Brighton a patient and not an active member of society.

She has a private room," the Doctor mentally noted. *"And personal clothing, plastic flowers, and a homemade quilt. It feels phony. She doesn't seem connected to anything around her. Nothing in the room is indicative of institutionalization or a person in transition.*

Her thoughts were broken by the sound of the older woman's voice.

"If you are looking for a tip, forget it. This is not a hotel." Kayla's expression became more focused. "The nurses think you're meaner than a rattlesnake. I wonder why?"

"Indeed."

Kayla narrowed her eyes. "You have an interesting accent. Where are you from?"

"If you are, in fact, a doctor, there should be files at your disposal to give you that information."

Kayla wandered through the room, running her finger across the top of the television stand. "I'd rather ask."

Mrs. Brighton shrugged and sipped her coffee. "Why are you here, Dr. Harris?"

She took a seat next to the bed on a rolling stool. "I just wanted to get to know you. I'll be your new psychiatrist. But I would like to think of me as your counselor."

"Counselor?" the patient said, impatience clear in her tone.

Kayla smirked as she stood up and walked back over toward the closed door. "Correct. I have a lot of letters behind my name. But I think you need a counselor more than a Psychiatrist."

Mrs. Brighton set the coffee down and eyed the young Doctor leaning against the wall.

"You're here to prove something," she said. "I am not inclined to help. The med nurse will be arriving soon. You should leave."

Kayla scribbled a note on her pad and said she would talk to her patient in a formal session another day. Once outside, she found the head nurse dispensing the morning medications to the residents of Hardaway. She made a mental note of the patient's observation skills. The little woman was very aware of her surroundings. And

"Dr. Harris," the nurse said. "How is your first day going so far?"

"So far, so good, Nurse Evans." Kayla smiled, clicking her pen on the notepad.

The nurse gave her an up and down look but stayed pleasant. "That's good. If you follow me, I'll show you the rest of this wing and how we operate."

"Thanks. I would appreciate that."

The nurse began to walk. "You were lucky she was in a generous mood this morning. Usually, we have to dodge anything we give her."

"Really? She is currently on a regimen of Lithium, Nardil, and Placidyl. She should be in a subdued state all the time." Kayla was reading from her notes.

The nurse gave Kayla a look of disbelief. "I don't think that woman has taken a full dose of that regimen in four years."

Kayla's brow furled. "Are you sure? How has she managed that?"

The nurse shrugged. "We can't prove that she doesn't take them because her lab work always says the drugs are in her system."

The nurse handed water, and some barbiturates to another resident.

"I heard one of the nurses mention her episodes," Kayla said. "Her chart mentions erratic behavior. It ranges from being quiet and withdrawn, to viciously aggressive."

"That about sums it up," the nurse said. "It happens daily in the spring."

"Interesting. Good thing I have two seasons to work on that. Is there anything else I should know?"

"Stay away from her curtains."

The rest of the day continued uneventful, and at the end of the day, Kayla sat down at her computer to record her notes. She had noticed that most of her patients were overmedicated. Kayla decided immediately to decrease their dosages to better understand how best to treat them individually. She worked on Mrs. Brighton's case last, especially since she wanted to devote a lot of time to her own special case.

It was obvious that Brighton had a lot of mental barriers and phobias brought on by depression. Mrs. Brighton had no previous history of mental illness but had had a mental breakdown of some sort and not recovered. Kayla's course of action would be simple: she would talk the woman down and get her off the meds. Three days later, an orderly walked Mrs. Brighton into Dr. Harris's office for their private session. The Doctor noted with curiosity the hateful look in the patient's cold glare. "Good afternoon, Mrs. Brighton."

"Good afternoon." The apathy in her patience's voice worried the Doctor.

Kayla frowned. "Where would you like to begin today? Anything you want to talk about, Alice?"

"On friendly terms so soon, even though I've declined to help you with your designs for greatness?"

"I don't know about greatness," Kayla gently replied. "I just want to help people."

Mrs. Brighton pushed her hair behind her ear with an air of indifference. "That is very noble of you. Tell me how you can help anyone if all you know is in black and white?"

Kayla glanced over and pointed with her pen. "I can tell you have a certain disdain for that orderly."

Mrs. Brighton rolled her eyes. "And a crow has wings."

"Why are you defensive, Alice?"

The older woman crossed her arms. "My happy pill quota has been altered. Am I a stone or a guinea pig?"

Kayla was quiet for a moment as she thought of the best response. An inexperienced therapist might analyze what Alice had just said, playing into the distraction.

"I would have you be neither," the Doctor finally replied. "But if you are one or the other, the lithium and the Nardil are doing little to help you, so you don't need them. Therefore, you are not a stone; neither are you stoned. However, the reduction in the Placidyl dosage should not induce defensive behavior. Besides, I am not testing you for side effects. Thus you are not my guinea pig. So, I ask again, why are you defensive?"

When she asked the question again, Kayla expected a change in body language, bordering on violence, or perhaps passive surrender. However, all she received was a glassy-eyed stare from her patient.

"A tower defends nothing; it merely watches," Alice began to recite. "And a guard is just a guard. Where have all the knights gone?"

Kayla didn't give in. "Riddles and poetry do not an answer make, Alice. It seems that you enjoy using wordplay to hide. You don't have to have to hide from me."

There was an odd rhythm in their conversation, as if they were dancing with words.

Had Kayla not been carefully observing her patient, she would have missed the slight smirk that graced her patient's thin lips. That was the last visible response that the Doctor received. Her patient had closed herself off. Guessing that Mrs. Brighton might like literature, Kayla used her laptop to search the internet for passages they could read together.

However, the counseling sessions became a one-sided recital as Alice maintained her indifference. As the hour came to a close, Kayla leaned back in her chair and gave a defeated sigh. The same orderly who had escorted Mrs. Brighton to the session rapped at the door. The old woman rose stiffly from her chair as the door was pushed open.

She took a step and then stopped. "Have you ever read 'Rumpelstiltskin' Doctor?"

"Not since childhood."

"Tell me my name, Dr. Harris, and I will consider answering your questions." The older woman padded out of the office, leaving a very confused doctor to ponder her parting words.

Kayla felt so defeated that she leaned back in her chair, staring at the ceiling. Her mind swung around the question, that smirk, her indignation. Kayla knew there was more to it, more than just a stubborn old woman.

Another tap on her door brought Kayla out of her daze.

"That looks very productive, Dr. Harris." Dr. Stephens cleared his throat.

Kayla let the chair come up so fast she nearly catapulted out of it. "Oh, hello, Dr. Stephens, what can I do for you?"

The Doctor gave her a phony smile. "Just came to check on you."

"Thank you. Dr. Stephens, I have a question about Mrs. Brighton. Has she ever shown any signs of dissociative disorder? I have read and reread her chart, but her behavior is Nothing like what I expected."

Dr. Stephens stepped further into the room and shut the door behind him. "Dr. Harris, you are new to this field. I want to give you some advice. There are patients here who need to be here, and there are some who don't. Some were put here because someone else mandated that they be here. And a few are here because they choose to be. Therefore, as doctors, we must choose wisely who to focus our energy on."

Kayla raised both eyebrows. "Are you saying I shouldn't focus on Mrs. Brighton because of her history?"

Dr. Stephens wasn't even trying to fake kind anymore. "I'm saying that there are other patients who would benefit more from your treatment methods than Alice Brighton."

Dr. Stephens left Kayla in an even more defeated state than he had found her in. She had been on the job only a few weeks and seemed to be hitting roadblocks at every turn with the Brighton case. Her other patients seemed to be doing better with the changes in their medications. The nurse was doing their best to adjust her methods, and some had already commented on the positive effects. Although a number of her patients did need the medication in addition to constant supervision, Mrs. Brighton was not in that percentile. Alice Brighton needed something else that Kayla could not put her finger on just yet.

* * * *

"Good morning, Mrs. Brighton. I brought you some coffee." Kayla was as cheerful as ever, but her cheer did little to change her patient's haughty disposition.

"It has been three days," the old woman said. "What have you to say to me?"

Kayla sipped her coffee and nodded. "About that, it dawned on me that Brighton is probably your married name, so I assume you would prefer to be called by your maiden name. The story you mentioned was written by the Grimm brothers. So, your name is Alice Grimm."

Alice rolled her eyes and stirred her drink. "To err is human."

Kayla had been proud to have come to that conclusion independently. Still, her ego was dealt a mild blow by the patient's reaction. "You answer to the name Alice. That must be your first name."

"Can a rose be anything other than a rose, if you call it by another name?"

Kayla pursed her lips. "You are talking in circles."

"Am I? That would be foolish."

Kayla was finding that Alice had succeeded in irritating her. She had only come to her room in the hope of getting a better dialogue going. The last thing the Doctor wanted was a repeat of the mime act that had taken place in her office.

"A fool is a prodigy in disguise," Kayla replied. "We can carry on this banter for the rest of the morning, Mrs. Brighton, but that is not productive."

Alice snuffed. "I have already informed you that I am not inclined to help you."

Kayla chuckled, contriving a means to gain control of the conversation. "That is unless I tell you your name."

There was a long pause, and all Kayla heard was the sound of her own swallowing. In the darkroom, she could hardly see the steel grey eyes boring into her.

Alice cleared her throat. "The med nurse will be coming with my Lithi—"

"No, she won't," Kayla cut in. "You don't need it in the morning. You're very calm and relaxed during this time of the day. You need it in the afternoon. To keep you relaxed for your group therapy."

"I don't have group therapy."

"You do now. I think it will help you." Kayla watched Alice raise her cup as if to throw it. "I recommend against doing anything hasty. There are three big burly orderlies outside, and they'll rush in here to restrain you if they hear anything out of the ordinary."

Alice sat back in her rocker. "Dr. Kayla Harris, you may be the good fairy in this fairy tale, but I will not be outdone."

Kayla blinked at the patient's strange refusal. Alice moved so quickly that Kayla had barely enough time to dodge the rain of hot coffee in the blink of the eye. The splatter made streaks on the wall, and droplets showered her white coat. But Kayla didn't see the coffee stains. She had curled into a defensive position as her patient's once docile hands changed into menacing claws.

Although Alice was not in the best physical shape, she quickly took advantage of the Doctor's automatic dodge. Just as she had been warned, the orderlies came charging in when they heard the Doctor's yelp. The men lifted the raging patient off the Doctor as if she were a bag of flour. The charge nurse ran in behind the orderlies, a syringe and vial of sedative in her hands.

Once the patient was sedated and restrained, Nurse Evans turned to the cowering young Doctor. "Are you all right, Dr. Harris?"

Green eyes shone in the dim light, showing a mixture of fear and shock.

"You have just been assaulted by your patient," the nurse continued, "with only a scratch to show for it. You should report this to Dr. Stephens."

Kayla rose mechanically obedient. She felt shaky, upset that she had let her guard down. The young Doctor had not expected the old woman to be so fast. Now she dreaded telling her superiors what had happened. It was her fault. She had pushed the patient too far. Kaila was so distraught about it that he told her to take a longer lunch when she reported to Dr. Stephens. It was clear from her attitude that Alice Brighton had won Round 2 of their on-going battle. She would be confined and restrained for a month. Kayla had a suspicion that Alice had known this would happen. Alice knew that an attack would keep her out of group therapy.

Kayla felt conflicted about Mrs. Brighton's punishment. She was a doctor, not a jailer. But what could she do? Rules were rules, and Alice was not above them. Even if she was very good at manipulating rules to accommodate her wants. Kayla planned to revisit her patient, but before doing so, she looked again at her personal records to get a better idea of who she was before she came to Hardaway.

The text simply said, "Divorcee: all claims sent to Mr. Douglas Brighton."

It took an Internet search to find the details in a local newspaper report: "Local Author Has Mental Breakdown."

The article reported that an "up and coming writer" had suffered "a mental breakdown due to sudden and bitter divorce from her husband of thirteen years, Douglas Brighton, producer and entrepreneur."

Mrs. Brighton had been sent to Hardaway Institution for evaluation. That had been eight years ago. The judge ordered that Douglas Brighton pay her medical bills as alimony. She felt confident that now she was armed for tomorrow's battle. Turning the computer off, Kayla went home with a faulty assumption.

* * * *

"Dr. Harris, how good of you to visit," Alice sang out, her voice filled with sarcasm. "That scratch has healed nicely. I was worried you got an infection or something."

Kayla sighed into her coffee, embarrassingly conscious of an invisible red line on her left cheek.

"Shouldn't Stephens be here to scold me or something?" Alice purposely rattled her restraints.

Kayla strolled over to the thick drapes and began toying with the hem of the fabric. "Rumpelstiltskin was a pixie of sorts, wasn't he, Alice?" Kayla waited for an answer she knew would not come. "All of those fairy creatures loved the light. They even did their dirty work in the day."

"What is your point?"

"Your vampire-like tendencies don't match your fey self-image," Kayla said, looking at the closed curtains.

"My dear girl, what a thing to say?! This is a psychiatric facility. You should watch your language." The old woman gave a sinister chuckle and smiled. "Lady, this is not some literary contest. It's real life. When I was a little girl, my father would talk about life like it was a joke. Then, if he was serious, he would say, 'You think these are jokes? It's real life.'"

"You know what your problem is?" Kayla said. "You're angry and bitter, and a list of other things I can't think of right now. But just because some man abandoned you, that doesn't mean you get to abandon yourself and hide from the world. That's just pathetic."

"Well, now, isn't this a well-versed analysis. This is out of character for you, Dr. Harris. Did someone get under your skin today?"

"I will make a deal with you, Alice. Attend a group counseling session twice a week. You don't have to participate. I just want you to behave yourself and get out of this room. The orderly will go away, and a female nurse will be assigned. No more restraints, and I'll take you off the lithium and Placidyl."

"How am I to endure without the white knight? Sir Tighty-Whiteys, my gracious captor. No, he must remain forever at my side. He shall accompany me always," Alice crooned with melodramatic fever. "Even as I go hither to yon privy."

The male nurse stood off to the side, ignoring the banter.

"Please, Alice, do this for me." Alice gazed at the Doctor with an owlish expression. "Why?"

"Because... Because...," Kayla struggled for a compelling comeback. "We both know this is not what you need. You can't honestly want this."

Alice yawned and leaned back into her pillows. "Sir Tighty-Whiteys, methinks the maiden dost jest. Look, how earnestly she doth imply she knows my nature. And yet she knows not my name. Come, fair maiden, and tell me my name, then I may grant ye a word."

Unable to tolerate Alice's mocking mood, the Doctor left her patient. They had come to another stalemate. All of her efforts were being met with theatrical resistance. Alice was so deep in her self-pity that the young Doctor was at a loss for how to break down the barriers she had erected around herself.

* * * *

The public library soon became Kayla's second refuge. It was where she could work at the riddle that was Alice Brighton. For six months, she had been questioning her sanity for indulging in Alice's delusions. She realized that the name issue was one thing Alice had become obsessed with during the last year. A proper name could be the one thing that stood between failure and success with Alice Brighton. So there Kayla sat, reading and rereading every fairy tale she could find. Besides the stacks of books was a notebook in which she recorded all the cross-references between Alice and fairy tales. But her conclusions and the lists she was making seemed ridiculous.

Then, just as she was packing up for the night, she caught a glimpse of something familiar. The library clerk was shelving the afternoon's returns in the children's section. The little green book on the top of the pile was the written version of Alice's delusion. Kayla picked up the book and started flipping through the pages. At the very back, she found the missing piece to her puzzle.

* * * *

"Good Morning, Charlene."

"What did you say?" The patient stopped mid-sip when the Doctor placed the picture book in her lap.

"I read about what happened to you, Charlene George. You were born in the U.S. Virgin Islands in 1961. You migrated to the States in 1976. Charlene married in 1979. You wrote youth fiction between 81 and 89. In 1992 you were divorced and admitted to Hardaway."

"Oh. That. It makes for a great tragedy. Don't you think? A story told a thousand times over." Charlene stopped her ramble to sip tea.

"Do you want to tell me your version of what happened?" Kayla asked. "The papers make it seem like George was a pseudonym."

Charlene gently stroked the cover of the book as if it were a delicate treasure. The usual sharp tongue retreated as she recounted her history.

"Hardly," she said. "Alice Brighton is the pseudonym. My husband thought my real name was too ethnic. Charlene Alicia George. That is what my mama named me. I married him and became Alice Brighton. I had to forget that I grew up among mango trees. Then I lost my taste for curry, and black cake to feed is his aspirations. That was two years after I had Aaron."

"That's enough for today," the Doctor said. "You don't have to tell me everything at once. I'll make sure the rest of the staff calls you Ms. George from now on."

"Kayla, will you open the curtains?" It was the first honest request Charlene George had made in years.

* * * *

Their sessions were much smoother after that. Kayla was able to talk to Charlene about the reasons for her pseudo-psychosis and the reality of her depression. Kayla convinced Charlene to do partner therapy with a girl nearly the same age as her real daughter. The foster relationship was beneficial to both patients well being. The positive results were also beneficial to Kayla's future career at Hardaway.

Another year rolled by, and spring was in the air. That year, Charlene didn't have an episode. However, the nurses still attested that she had a sour disposition. One breezy April morning, Charlene and one of the nurses tap on Dr. Harris's door. Charlene wanted to go outside for their morning talk.

They strolled along quietly at first, then, when the nurse left them alone, Kayla initiated a casual conversation. "The reports from your group session say that you have been interacting."

Alice scoffed. "The sprites think I'm their mother. I am no one's mother."

"Dr. Gupta says you have a positive effect on them, Charlene. And you are someone's mother. But I'm thrilled with the progress you've made. Dr. Stephens has even commented about you."

Charlene tensed slightly at the mention of the head doctor.

"I know you don't like him much. I know he can be a hard pill to swallow. That, and he is another man controlling your life. However, I believe that your distrust of the opposite sex will fade with time," Kayla said. "Just think to yourself, 'the man in front of me is not my husband. This person deserves a chance.'"

Charlene took a deep breath. "It wasn't so upsetting that he left me or took my money. It hurt when Henry took my children from me. I gave him everything, and he left. I had our problems, like all couples. It felt like he did it just because he could. As if I was just an object, he was tired of possessing."

She paused, taking a deep breath before continuing. "I raised my children with love. Taught them they should love both of us while we were going through the separation. But, somehow, that insincere man poisoned their minds in one week. They came home after their with him with sour attitudes. Called me horrible things and demanded to be with their father. The Custody battle was a nightmare. Sora And Theo cried, begging the judge to give their father sole custody. "

Charlene paused again, seeming to be reliving that awful day.

Kayla waited silently for Charlene to continue.

"Henry made ups such lies. I had assured my lawyer that it was going to be civil and we'd have joint custody. Neither of us was prepared. The courts sided with Henry and his falsehoods. That's why I cracked."

"I have kept you long enough," the old woman said. "The reason I asked you out here is not to rant about life. I want to leave."

"Are you Hesure you're ready?"

Charlene took a deep breath. "No, but I don't need to be here any longer. Perhaps it's time I made a phone call or two."

"Who will you call?" Kayla was curious.

"God, first of all, and I'll thank Him for sending you to me. Then a call to someone who was once good to me."

Kayla stopped and stared at her. "Charlene, I think you just said something nice."

Charlene rose from the bench without another word. Kayla barely stifled a chuckle as she watched her patient being ushered back to her room.

* * * *

Charlene requested an appointment with Dr. Stephens to discuss her status at Hardaway Institute.

"Well, Mrs. Brighton," the head doctor said. "I see no reason why you should not be able to rejoin society. You checked yourself in, and you can check yourself out. I trust you have someplace to return to?"

"Yes, Dr. Stephens, I do. And please call me by my maiden name."

The Doctor nodded, making a note. "Well, it seems to me you have been working on this for some time. However, I am going to have to ask that you seek regular counseling outside."

"Of course. Doctor, am I excused?"

He gave her a quick look and nodded. "Yes. Good day, Ms. George."

Charlene walked out slowly, almost unsure of her footing. The uncertainty of what lay ahead suddenly felt heavy. She had made her phone calls, the second harder than the first. She was both surprised and relieved when Thomas Funderburke answered her call. Thomas had been her closest friend. Now she needed him again. He did not disappoint her. They spoke as if 10 years had not separated them. He enthusiastically helped Charlene make arrangements to rejoin the world. Charlene was moving to a place she had thought she would never see again. She was starting over in the same place where her journey had begun.

Dear Kayla,

First, I would like to apologize for not saying farewell in person. I don't want to say goodbye to you; I know we are not friends. That is unrealistic. You were doing your job, and for that, I am grateful. Know that I do feel an affinity towards you, so you will be missed.

Dr. Stephens wants me to seek another counselor when I arrive at my next destination, so you will probably receive reports soon. I promise to keep them interesting. If you would like to contact me, the address is enclosed, along with a copy of my new manuscript. I hope you can read it to those sprites. They might enjoy it.

Sincerely,
Charlene A. George

Bend

I can't believe that I'm on a rooftop. It's cold, windy, and I'm on a rooftop. I can't believe I agreed to this. To be cold and super flexed in this position was not what I agreed to."

"Millie," Deshawn said, standing over her, holding her knees over her head, "you need to focus on breathing, or you're going to pass out."

"Easy for you to say," she grunted. "This is only a stretching position. I am doing all the hard work."

Millie grew quiet and tried to focus on what Deshawn had instructed her to do. Breathe slowly in through the mouth and out of the nose. Focus only on the sound of her breathing while mentally recanting how she had arrived in the position she found herself in.

* * * *

I should be in church on Sunday. Not on a roof breathing!

Deshawn had been pestering her for weeks to let him get the stress knots out of her neck and shoulders. She had expected a massage, not yoga. Millie didn't know the first thing about yoga, only that it involved a lot of obscene posing. Getting a massage from a coworker seemed equally risquè She was incredibly reluctant to allow Deshawn to do anything for her outside of the job. Even before she found out that he intended to put her through a grueling exercise session. But the tension in her shoulders was getting worse. She thought back to their conversation a week ago.

"You carry a lot of unnecessary tension for someone who says their job is not brain surgery," he had said.

"Umm... You think I am tense?"

Deshawn had started nodding before she had even finished her sentence. "Yes. There isn't some rule about fraternizing outside of work, is there?

She thought for a moment before responding. "No, Mr. Funderburke is very liberal. He thinks we should have as many positive interactions amongst the staff as possible to promote team morale."

"Great, come by my studio next Sunday morn—"

Millie held up her hand quickly cut him off. "I have church."

Deshawn grabbed the last envelope from her, squaring her with an unapologetic look.

"God exists everywhere, in everything, and fellowship is not limited to a pew," He stated flatly.

Deshawn's assertion had left Millie mildly unsettled. His statement was filled will rock-solid resolve, followed with a hint of irritation that he even had to say it. But Millie could not remember when she had not found her way to the Holy House.

Millie's aunts call the church that, and she found herself saying it all these years later.

She had never proclaimed to be sanctified and holy. However, she understood what it meant to have faith in the Lord. The thought Deshawn had presented her with was not foreign. She had heard people say it before, and to a degree, she believed it herself. However, she couldn't justify not going to service. The rest of the week went by without either of them mentioning the topic again.

Millie woke up at dawn Sunday morning. Although not a habitual early riser, she took it as a sign of being rested. Stretching, she set about getting her day started. One of her curlers was even more anxious to get going and had escaped her bonnet. The stay was quickly retrieved and placed in the bag of others tied to her closet door. Also hanging from her closet door was a sharply pressed suit she had taken out the night before. It was burgundy colored two-piece that she paired with a cream sweater and matching beret in the winter. She even had specific garnet and gold jewelry set to go with it. The high polished pumps in just the right shade to match the suit were waiting in their box to be donned. It was one of her most coordinated outfits and, therefore, her favorite. Fingering the material, she reflected on the time she put into putting the garments together. The usual pride she felt when looking at the outfit was replaced with a feeling of triviality.

Shaking the feeling way, she opted for the shower. Hoping that the warm water would invigorate her with more positive thoughts.

Getting dressed, she still felt a sense of ennui about putting on her clothes. The curlers were in their box, but she was reluctant to tease her thick coils into style.

A quiet voice whispered in her head said, *you want to see something different.*

Normally, she would have said, "The devil is a liar," and clothed herself in that beautiful suit and marched into Trinity Baptist. But doing that did not seem important. Oddly her spirit was not conflicted. It was at peace with her taking a different path. Grabbing her phone, she scrolled the contacts and found Deshawn's number. She texted him a quick message.

GOOD MORNING. IS YOUR INVITATION STILL OPEN?

The instant she hit send, she began to worry if she had done the right thing. But before she could recall the message, her phone chimed.

Yes. Come by around 10. Wear something you can move in.

Something I can move in? She thought, only now realizing he had described what he had planned in his studio. Diving into her chest of drawers, Millie found a forgotten tracksuit. She remembered a pair of unworn sneakers in the back of the closet. She pulled those on too. Lastly, she considered what to do with her hair. It has taken hours to roll it. Quickly, she brushed, wrapped, and tied down her hair. Outfit assembled, she gave herself a once over in the mirror. The image caused her to laugh. It was not an everyday look for her. *Haha, look at me, Gym rat, Millie.* She thought while looking in the mirror. It felt like a costume, but it would be easy to move around in, so it meets the criteria.

Millie quietly said a prayer, read her scripture and devotional of the day before leaving. She rolled pulled the sedan out of the highrise garage, destined for Deshawn's Studio. Plugging the address into her GPS, she headed away from her normal Sunday course. She ventured to a part of the city she rarely visited. During the cruise through light morning traffic, she considered turning around at several stoplights. There was still time for her to get back to her normal routine. There was no shame in realizing that this may be too far out of her element. They were still supervisor to trainee dynamic; this wasn't exactly a team-building exercise. As the excuses formed, she could also hear Deshawn's counter-argument. She also found it funny that her subconscious was turning Deshawn into the devil on her shoulder.

Her window to run closed when the door had opened.

Deshawn had pulled her inside and seated them at his kitchen table before she could say anything.

"You look cold," he had said. "I have some tea."

Tea together started fine. Nice casual conversation, nothing out of the ordinary, until Deshawn grabbed her wrist and started bending and moving it. Millie was perplexed, and her face must have shown it because when he looked at her again, he laughed heartily.

"Millie," he had said, "you are going to have to relax and have an open mind if we are going to get through this morning."

He took a closer look at the tracksuit she was wearing and nodded approvingly.

"Let's get started."

* * * *

How was she supposed to feel relaxed on the roof and in an upside-down fetal position? All the exercise proved that she was not completely inflexible in her old age, but it was not the most relaxing thing she had ever done. Deshawn was laughed so hard she was starting to think this was a plot to embarrass her.

"I can't believe I let you talk me into this," she said. She couldn't tell if the bun she had tightly fixed to her head was a help or hindrance.

"Can you even do half the stuff you're making me do?"

"That and more. Sit up and observe."

As Millie watched, Deshawn sprang into action, moving in a fluid secession of poses. She suddenly felt jealous, a sentiment rooted in the fact that she never looked that content and focused simultaneously. After Deshawn's exhibition, they stayed on the roof a while longer, and Millie finished the routine with fewer protests. By the time the noon sun started to warm the concrete garden, teacher and student were winding down.

"You must be hungry," he said. "You should stay for lunch."

At first, Millie protested, but a gurgling in her stomach made her sit at the table and shut up. Deshawn gave her a wink and went into the kitchen, leaving her to explore the loft. The table she sat at was nestled between the kitchen and a set of stairs. The stairs that led to the bedroom over her head. To her left was the living area. Which had gone unnoticed until that point, hidden behind the bookcase and the secretary beside the door.

"I hope you're not getting bored at the office," she said, taking in the sweeping view of the city from his living room windows.

"No," he replied. "I just didn't realize how much correspondence went into a publication. To be honest, I started this internship just so I could get the extra nod for when I entered the broadcasting field."

Millie looked over at the small table against the wall. "Is that so? Hey, where did you get all these masks?"

He talked loudly from the other room. "My girl's in Africa. She sends a mask home occasionally. I'm house-sitting until she makes an honest man out of me."

Pulling utensils out of drawers, he looked over his shoulder and saw Millie staring out the window. "Would you believe that five years ago, this whole neighborhood was a slum? Gentrification has worked wonders for this place."

"I heard about it on the news," Millie replied, "but I didn't really believe it. I don't frequent this side of town."

He set their drinks and lunch on the table.

"I thought you would be health nut after this morning," she said, giving their spread a critical look.

"Nope, I believe in moderation. Would you believe I used to smoke? Two packs of Newport's a day. But Valeria didn't like it. I quit cold turkey after a year with her."

"What is she doing in the Motherland?" Deshawn swallowed hard.

"She is on her way to becoming a doctor. But that's on hold. No thanks to the influence of her old roommate. You know the type; ponytail wearing, artsy, and out there. Anyway, she decided to join the Peace Corps. For a year before doing her residency. Now she's in West Africa building wells and teaching kids to read." Mille heard notes of resentment in his tone and tried to focus the conversation on the situation's good.

"Valerie's doing good work. Why didn't you go? That kind of work would have gotten you references, too."

"I did go for a week. I couldn't handle it. Then Katrina hit. It was easier for me to come back and help the clean-up effort here than to see the look on some of those kids' faces."

Millie's eyes wandered off for a moment. "On the T.V., they always seem really hurt or really happy."

Deshawn suddenly sounded so passionate. "That's the T.V. magic. On the one hand, you go thinking you can help. Then you get there and realize the problem is more than poverty and the remnants of colonialism. Local and international complacency and negligence keep those kids in an endless cycle that a couple of U.S. cents a day aren't going to fix. And despite those odds, they still have hope. It was too damn eerie."

"Deshawn, sometimes I forget that you have so much experience. At thirty, all I did was move here and start my job."

Millie didn't like the guilty feeling that was starting to develop in her gut. The topic was too heavy. The wicked problems of the world always did this to her. She didn't like not having a solution. Understanding that she may be apart of the system that propagated such ugliness did not sit well either.

"That's not a bad thing," he said between bites of his sandwich.

"Maybe not to you. But every now and again, I meet people who make me feel like I haven't done anything with my life," she admitted quietly.

"You just need to relax," he said. "You don't have to go around the world to experience life. If we learn to appreciate what we have, everyone gets some part of the joy of living."

Millie pointed her fork at him accusingly. "Thanks for the words of wisdom, Great Sage."

She smiled.

Deshawn shook his head. "It's all Val's bad influence."

Millie wrinkled her nose. "You miss her?"

He sighed and shrugged his shoulders. "Yeah, but I guess I'll have to make do with you until she gets back."

He was too busy with his lunch to notice that Millie's eyes had grown as big as saucers, and she had stopped breathing. Only when he asked her if she liked the quinoa went unanswered did he look up again. He laughed at her expression. "Millie, breathe! I was joking."

Millie put her hand to her chest, furrowing her brow. "What you said was inappropriate."

"I wish I had a camera out." He continued to chuckle. "That face is priceless."

She scowled at him. "It isn't funny."

"See? You need to loosen up. Just be glad I'm not like I was in my heyday. A woman like you... Well, let's just I was not always a good guy."

Millie stared blankly at the mask on the wall behind his head. "What do you mean a woman like me?"

Deshawn put his fork down, taking in Millie's determined defense look yet.

"I'll answer your questions. But, remember, you opened the door."

"Continue," she said pointedly, squaring her shoulders to show she was ready for what he had to dish out.

"You have a very fixed façade. You behave, speak, and dress in a manner that makes it clear that you are the quintessential well-educated black woman—a Black Southern Belle. I know the type well. You grow up with your mind revolving around the church, cotillions, college, and marriage. What you are really striving for is social acceptance. You are constantly trying to prove yourself to groups of individuals that you fit into their ideal".

He paused, leaning forward, his eyes never leaving hers. "The women that are created from that environment are formidable. But underneath all of that rigidity of social propriety, they want to be… surprised. They want to feel free. I have a keen ability to find what that type of woman wants to be surprised with".

"So that why you asked me here? To surprise me?"

"No, Millie, remember I said I used to be that kind of guy, playing on the unspoken wants of sheltered women. But, when Valeria walked into my life, things changes. You are here because I had a cancellation and could use a deep stretch. You must have overlooked the certified yoga instructor part in my cover letter".

Again, he had exceeded her expectations. Millie dumbstruck. She liked this guy a little more every time they spoke.

"You remind me of a conversation I overheard in my favorite restaurant," she finally said. "The two men talking seemed like the metrosexual type, so I dismissed them as a family and tried to ignore their chat. But at some point, I began to tune into what they were saying. They weren't family; it turns out that one was a man of faith and the other a shrewd businessman. The man of faith was having problems with his personal … well, his love life. It sounded like he was in love with one woman, but he just couldn't seem to avoid cheating on her. Even though he knew it was wrong. He said that it was childish that he ought to know better at his age but couldn't seem to stop himself. "

Millie shifted in her chair, recalling the rest of the story.

"He sounded sincerely apologetic about hurting the woman that had his heart. The businessman seemed to know the couple very well. He never took sides. He just laid it on the line. And I want to say that he said something like… 'well, you commit yourself to a lot of things in your life. Things like your work and church, but it's hard to commit to a person. it's hard because you can't predict what that person will say or do during your relationship; that's why you have issues."

She paused with a shrug of her achy shoulders before continuing.

"Their conservation went on about several things that I don't remember. By the time they left, I had developed a new respect for the modern brother. And I guess you remind me of them. You're at the point in your relationship that that dude was trying to reach. But if you weren't in this space, I would be… I going to say prey to you."

Deshawn grinned.

"You can put it like that. But unlike that guy, I didn't want a relationship. I loved the game. I liked seeing those women crumble when I walked away. And some of them were even more fun to watch as they rebuilt themselves."

"That does make you sound like a Villain."

"Yeah, I was an asshole, no lie. Then Valeria showed up and decided I wanted to… no, needed to be a better man".

"You whipped?" Millie joked.

"Happily. Val's the one, and she knows it."

Not knowing how else to respond, Millie shrugged. Maybe Deshawn had a point. Maybe she did need to loosen up. But the question was how much, and did that mean more rooftop yoga sessions? And if it did, would she be able to endure the throbbing of her sore muscles?

* * * *

The Winters holidays could not come fast enough for Deshawn. Valeria had phoned to say she was coming home soon with a big surprise. She would not give him any clue, and he made anxious. He was afraid that she would decide to stay overseas indefinitely. But he would not let unfounded worry consume his thoughts. He still needed to focus on work. Millie had assured him that he had a long enough break to enjoy plenty of time with his globe-trotting lover. Unfortunately, that meant she would work him to death as they pushed to get ahead before the New Year.

Thoughts of how he would spend his days with Valerie swirled through his thoughts as he arrived at the office. Shaking the snow from his boots and dusting his head, Deshawn started up the stairs to the editing department.

He thought back to the first time he heard about the publishing house. Thunder Press was a fairly new and small operation. It focused on helping new and local authors improve and publish their work. The grassroots organization style surviving in a large city and changing industry intrigued him. He loved media in all its forms and wondered how the company was transitioning and adapting to the digital age. When he was interviewed by founder Thomas Funderburke, that topic had taken up most of the conversation. By the end of their discussion, Deshawn was certain that not only did he land the position but that he would be working with Funderburke directly. But, Funderburke had other plans. Much to Deshawn's chagrin, he would be on probation for a year, working in the divisions of the Press before he would finish in his position.

For what it was worth, it wasn't as bad as he'd initially thought it would be. The bulk of his tasks centered around helping Millie and Charlene shed their unhealthy aversion to technology and social media. He learned a lot by having to deal with Millie's "electrical correspondence," as she put it. He learned the office jargon quickly and helped with a lot of projects before being asked. Being able to create the illusion that he was always a step ahead. Secretly, he found it very entertaining to watch his supervisors apprehensively make posts on social media.

Getting used to all the personalities in the department had been the hard part. Tanya had been the first to warm up to him. They work well together. She gave him all the tips tricks for their department and the others he would be migrating to later on.

Thought Millie and how she would describe her. It would sound like he was giving a professional referral. Millie is well spoken, well educated, and career-orientated. She likes everything in its proper place. She is also very analytical, a classic A-type personality. Those were the qualities that allowed her to excel as an editor. She had all the charm and wit to keep clients and employers happy. Side note: the idea of being carefree is as foreign to her as riding a camel down the main street of her hometown.

That last thought made him snicker up the stairs.

Upon entering their corner of the company, he hung his coat and scarf on the rack and waved at Tanya. Then Thomas and Charlene emerged from her office with a jovial air. When Charlene realized they had an audience, she immediately frowned.

"Tanya," Thomas crooned. "What a lovely sight you are this morning. How are you?"

"Good morning to you too, Mr. Funderburke" Tanya, replied with a smile. It was just Thomas Funderburke's standard greeting for every woman he met. No need to call H.R.

Then he noticed Deshawn. "It's good to see you too, Deshawn."

Deshawn returned his greeting.

"Where's Millie?" Thomas asked, looking around like he lost something. "She's usually here by now."

"She is running late," Tanya said. "The traffic is really bad on her side of town."

"A fact of life; People freak out when there's moisture on the road. Anyway, I came to remind everyone of the holiday schedule and to announce that this year we will have a New Year's party." The publisher turned to Tanya. "Here are the event plans. Please make sure that our non-in-house people and these clients get a copy. Alright, then." He flashed another smile at his employees. "I'll be in my office if you need me."

He disappeared upstairs.

Deshawn turned to greet Charlene, only to receive a curt nod before she retreated into her office. Charlene was a character he could not figure out. There were rumors all over the office about her night and day behavior. However, he did like any on the office scuttlebutt theories. Instead, he focused his energy on maintaining the department's sense of harmony. In an office with such a unique dynamic, he learned that when Charlene decided it was a nonverbal day to stick to Millie and Tanya until otherwise directed.

He darted into Millie's office, set about his morning objectives. He pulled out the reference books and started taking notes that would be passed on to one of Millie's clients. However, after a few moments, he felt uncomfortable. *She's really late, there must have been an accident.*

He moved from his chair to Millie's desk. But he was still uncomfortable. Putting his pen down, Deshawn stood up and paced the room. After five minutes of that, he still could not decide what was making him uncomfortable. But time was slipping away, and Deshawn needed to finish up his assignment. He started rearranging their workspace. He happened upon the large package. But hesitant to open it. It has been there longer than he. And maybe she had her reasons for leaving it there.

Millie arrived an hour later. By the time she walked into the foyer, it had stopped snowing. Now that she had made it to work safely, Tanya gave her the messages, and Deshawn stopped fidgeting.

Maybe, I was just worried, he said to himself.

* * * *

After the New Year's party, Deshawn decided to rearrange Millie's office as a present. The room needed better flow, and he knew a little Feng Shui would help. Or so Valeria suggested. It would be a more valuable gift than some trinket. He let Tanya in on his plan at the party. She immediately agreed to help and suggest they do it the morning they returned to work,

As they moved things around, Deshawn couldn't help but notice that Tanya was very excited about moving one item in particular. It was the oversized box Millie had stored in the corner months before. When they pulled the box out of the corner, Deshawn and Tanya were surprised to find a painting inside. After they hung it, they stood awkwardly side by side, staring at it, stupefied.

"What are you two up to?" Millie's voice came from behind them.

"Millie," Tanya asked. "When did you have a portrait commissioned?"

Millie had come to a halt when they saw what they were looking at. All she could gape and shake her head.

"I didn't know the model for this."

Unable to read her body language, Deshawn asked, "Millie, are you upset? We can put it back."

Tanya was still looking at the painting. "But that's you, right? Why would some random person just paint you ... like that?"

The question spurred Millie out of her daze, and she began looking around the room anxiously. When her eyes rested on the packaging, there was a rush to get it in her hands. Clutching the remnants of the box, she read out the name of the sender.

She stuttered out, "Tipinianca... T... P... Taylar P. Nianca!"

The color seemed to drain from Millie's face as she looked at the painting again.

Deshawn rolled a chair out for her. "Are you sure it's from this Nianca person?"

"Yes, I'm sure. Nianca is not a common name. I saw an exhibition of artists calling themselves Les peintures révolutionnaires. They toured ten cities doing different projects. They came to Savannah with the Intimacy Project. Twelve artists presenting twelve paintings of the things their model considered an intimate gesture. And twelve images of things they didn't think were intimate."

"Only the French would think up a traveling porn show," Tanya snorted.

Millie laughed. "Sex is an immature idea of intimacy. Does Taylar's portrait of me have anything to do with sex?"

Deshawn looked more closely at the portrait. "No. , But it looks like Taylar knew or saw a side of you we don't know about. But still ... why are you so upset?"

"So, who is this, Taylar?" Tanya asked. "He's your ex-boyfriend, huh?"

Millie's starry-eyed daze baffled and worried her coworkers. It took her few moments to answer either of their questions. She was transfixed by memories from her youth dancing behind her eyes.

Finally, she said, "Ex-boyfriend? Former Mistress? Friend? Teacher? Artist? Explorer? Taylar is not easy to describe. Taylar is Taylar."

"So, what does that make Taylar to you?" Deshawn asked.

Millie turned to him. "At first, Taylar was just another subject for the campus paper. But in two days, eleven hours, twenty minutes, and sixteen seconds, I fell in love. And then Taylar was gone. The group didn't know where their partner went. However, they did have Taylar's pieces for the next four cities."

She looked at the painting longingly before turning away again. "They let me see the rest of the collection. It's amazing what people let you get away with when they think they have an angry black woman on their hands. I memorized every brush stroke. This portrait was not among them. Truth be told, I was angry for a long time. All because I forgot the first thing Taylar told me. 'If you can trust, you can love. That's the path to true intimacy. Therefore, when you trust, do so wholeheartedly, and if that trust becomes love, accept it for everything it is worth, even it lasts for only a moment.' I got over it. Then I stopped thinking about Taylar Nianca again. But right now, for some strange reason, I want to cry."

The room grew quiet. This was not the reaction Deshawn was hoping for. Tanya broke the silence.

"Wow, that's deep," said Tanya.

No one noticed Charlene standing in the doorway, listening. She stepped forward. "Millie, I am going to nominate you to be the travel writer for the new magazine. It's time you expanded your horizons."

"Where did you come from, Charlene?" Millie asked, wiping her eyes.

Charlene kept her eyes glued on Millie. "You've become a little lackluster. It's time to get out of this box."

"But, Charlene," Tanya said, "she has to go through reviews and the portfolio. And what about her work ..."

Charlene put up her hand. "I am aware of that, Tanya. I can handle the majority of it. But I have to have Mr. Clemons remain in our department to assist until we can replace Millie. In the meantime, Millie, you should start packing."

"Hold on, I have not to desire to leave my position or move. That magazine is North Carolina. Not trying to go back down south."

"Millie, this is a great opportunity. You should take it. You want to know why that painting makes you want to cry. It's because the woman on the other side of that mirror is living. She is you, and you don't know her."

Charlene folded her arms, waiting for Millie to say something. A confirmation or a denial would have suited Charlene, but she did want silence.

"Sprites, I think we should leave Ms. Jackson to her ruminations," Charlene turned on her heels, expecting Deshawn and Tanya to follow.

Reluctantly they left; Tanya offered an apology as they went.

Inside Millie was a torrent of emotions. Charlene had struck a nerve. She didn't want to admit it. Millie did not want to say, but she fantasized about what nontraditional work looked like. She did not want to admit that maybe she had unresolved feels for someone she barely knew. Or that she sometimes prayed for excitement in her life.

Excitement had knocked on her door.

In Search Of

It had not occurred to me that it's been so long, and yet I remember every second. Every second I was in your presence.

A shower had become a rainstorm, flooding some distant back-alley art district. There, the beatniks and bohemians still met, alongside the techno-geeks and aging entrepreneurs. Through the dense veil of falling water, the soft glow of an open café lit the street. There was a party in one of the upper flats. Music floated down, barely audible over the downpour. It was no tourist trap. No real tourists ever went there. It was too foreign, too far off the beaten path. Only the locals went there, and if you could blend in, you were more than welcome.

Why am I still looking? That person is laughing at me, I know. 'Our emotions transcend time and space, and the receiver should get the message, just like e-mail.' If that's true, then that person is definitely laughing.

Standing under a lone streetlight, a figure wrapped in a wet trench coat was checking soggy directions. The evening had begun with a cool refreshing shower, which was followed by a nighttime squall. The directions gave little information, so the reader stuffed them away without hesitation.

All those years, and not a word, not a smoke signal, nothing. Then one day, out of the blue ... you... you just reenter my life. You would say, 'Our emotions are intangible. It's the memory from which our emotions stem that makes those feelings meaningful.' Philosophical nonsense! I am tired of grasping at memories! I need to know it was real.

The place was like a hundred others. The globe could be condensed into back alleys like that one. Everything that could be bought or experienced transpired in places like that. The café was starting to close, allowing the darkness of night to seep out of the margins. The streetlamp felt like the sun, a lone beacon against the void. Its light neutralized the black holes produced by enormous puddles. The trench coat moved on in aimless abandon. The end of the road came in the blink of an eye. Three streets over, the beaten path was in plain sight, but there were no treasures over there, only trinkets for those who would mistake the falling rain for falling stars. There was a distant flicker in the void, a forgotten star, a lonely twinkle that beckoned the Seeker away from complacent mediocrity.

Our time together seemed so wondrous, almost infinite. We were in search of grand aspirations in those youthful days; I wonder if you found everything you wanted. My path wants to entwine with yours. Perhaps, I have become needy, or selfish to hunt for you this way.

The trench coat traveled the path to that faint star. Its window was large enough for mannequins garbed in strange costumes to parade among crafts and photographs. Then there it was, found in the moment when all hope was lost. But the light was fading. It was still raining and time was slipping away. The door was tried. It was locked. The Seeker began to bang on the door in desperation, shouting in four languages, hoping that one of them would be heard and understood.

Divine intervention turned the lights back on. An older man came to the door with an irate look on his face. His solicitor pointed and pled with elated hope and the fear of disappointment. The owner scarcely cared that the plane was leaving in the morning, didn't care that the directions had not been clear, that the search had taken ages.

But through the chatter, he could hear clearly. "I know the artist."

The old man unlocked the door. He was saluted like a king for his trouble.

The owner motioned to his guest to sit and locked his door again. The rain was subsiding. The world was slowing down. The owner listened to the story in its entirety. He brought the painting forward and placed it on an easel to be examined. The owner said he didn't know its origin, but that its title was Ayala. His guest smiled. There were tears of joy.

After so long, I've found something of you?

The owner prepped his register. The guest gave him two cards: one plastic, one with an address. The guest thanked the owner one last time. Tears rolled against a broadening smile. The door had a little bell whose soft jingle had been nullified by the noise of the storm. The bell had a pleasant jingle. The kind of sound that should awaken someone from a dream. The storm gave way to the bright moon, heralding the end of the journey.

Arrangements

Aisha sat in her favorite coffee shop for her lunch break. She by the window reanalyzing the plans she has implemented since shipping her dogs to Mint Hill.

It's messed up. How did it come to this? I was so close. It's better this way. Now I got to tell Ms. Elly that She was right and I should move into the house. I send all my time here anyway. my lease is about up, so the timing works out.

Ms. Elly won't mind too much. She's in a nice nursing home, and I've seen to it that all her finances are taken care of. When poor Miss Elly took to wandering and forget- ting things, I couldn't leave her alone in that big house. She likes Rolling Green, and the staff is on point. That good-for-nothing ex of mine getting locked up for ten to twenty was one of the highlights of my life. The situation gives me more time with my surrogate mom. I always liked visiting Ms. Elly. As far as she's concerned, I can do no wrong. My mom was always spit and nails with me, but with Ms. Elly, it was always, 'Aisha, baby, you want honey on ya biscuits?' I miss when she'd make them just for me, even after I and that fool split up. If Rodney had watched his back, Ms. Elly wouldn't have had to call me. 'Aisha, baby, Rodney in trouble and done left me here with the dogs. And dese boys have been callin' to the house looking for him.' Luckily, I know most of those jokers, and Baja knew Patches, and next thing I know, I am dealing in puppies.

Anyway, it's time I close that chapter. But I have to admit that this final smokescreen to throw off the feds might be a bit much. Taking on a roommate is a little extreme. I even skipped some monthly bills just to make it look like I'm struggling. I got rid of the prepaid phone, so no worries there. Watching spy movies came in handy. I think that is everything. I built Doris and Shell a kennel in the backyard. I'll just have to take them to a park. Wait a minute. Is that who I think it is?

Aisha watched in disbelief as the man she did not want to see again emerge from a parked van. He jogged across the street and into the coffee shop. She continued watching the parking lot, hoping that the agent's appearance had nothing to do with her. Unfortunately, that hope was dashed when a familiar form slid into the seat across from her.

"You never called," he said with a hint of mischief.

The play in his voice almost made Aisha think she had jumped the gun.

Maybe he isn't a fed. But she dismissed the thought. She trusted her instincts.

Ulysses leaned back to watch Aisha leave. As he enjoyed the view of her swaying hips, his Bluetooth buzzed.

"Why are you following her? You're not even supposed to be out in the open."

"The view is lovely. Besides, doing something like that won't do us any good."

"She's the reason all the targets have gone to ground.

Someone else can bring her in for questioning."

"Relax." Ulysses grinned into his coffee cup. "There is a better way to do what needs doing. They'll resurface, but in the meantime, let me worry about the lady."

"You're lucky you have not been shipped back to Tennessee."

Ulysses ended the call and sank into the chair. He wasn't about to let the chain of command stress him out. The handlers were impeding his hunt, with all their unnecessary restrictions. He had the investigation under control, despite this minor hang up.

Aisha hurried back to her office. Revising and upload- ing her ad for a roommate had just moved up to priority one. The first line read, "Must love dogs."

The following weeks were a blur of faces and names. In addition to her inability to choose a roommate. She also had to endure the stress of her mother's nagging. She encountered argument after argument. Her mother insisted that she would be giving up her precious privacy and that if she wanted a roommate so bad, she should move back home. And if Ms. Shirley had not run that in ground, she said that it was just foolish, more times than Aisha could count. Telling Mom the truth behind her actions was out of questions, so Aisha maintained a simple defense: she could pay off the house faster with the extra money. Besides, she had two over-protective guard dogs, so her security would not be a question. After a lot of bickering and fussing, her mother finally gave up and decided to ignore her daughter's latest fiasco.

Six weeks later, Aisha took one more application. The applicant sent a fax containing references, a copy of credit history, and a list of questions. Aisha instantly liked this one. She phoned Ms. Johnson immediately. Three days later, Millie met with Aisha at her favorite coffee shop. They were well suited for each other.

The Magazine was stationed in the North Carolina. A place Millie did never expected to live. And not knowing how long she would be there didn't want to rush into buying a new home. When she learned about Aisha's rental space it seemed like the perfect compromise. She would not have all the added responsibilities of owning property; while dealing with the stresses of being a trans- plant resident and adjusting to a new work environment. Living with another working professional, was just what she needed.

They had the same conclusions about each other as the interview progressed. They approached the situation like the Camp David Accord, in order to maintain each other autonomy. Two mocha lattes later, Aisha was driv- ing home with a passenger. Inside the house, they were greeted by Doris, who gave Millie a warning growl, while Shell remained curled up in his bed. Aisha quickly inter- vened and the let Doris meet Millie, who cautiously let the huge dog sniff her hand and decide if they were going to be friends or not. Aisha watched hopefully. Two other candidates had been scared off by Doris's size. But Millie did not appear to be intimidated. "Doris," she said, pet- ting the animal, "be nice to this prospective roommate." Soon enough, Doris snorted and lumbered off to retrieve her chew toy.

Millie smiled "She's friendly. Can we continue the tour?"

"Sure. There's a gourmet kitchen and formal dinning room down the hall on the left. The dogs are not allowed in there. The washer and dryer are under the stairs. We will only share this floor."

"The den seems bare. Do you mind if I put my media stuff in there?"

"No, but I usually put Doris and Shell in there at night."

"They aren't going to hump on my couch, are they?"

"No. Shell is neutered, and Doris goes outside during that time. Do you want to see the mother –in-law suite now?" When Millie nodded, Aisha led her through the kitchen to a door leading to the ground level garage.

Millie's suite was a good size for someone starting over. She had a bedroom, a closet, a bathroom, and some open space. Sharing the kitchen would be fine, and she had somewhere to watch her movies. The house was a contemporary cookie cutter with too much space for one person. Millie was sold.

Millie and Aisha agreed on three-month trial to see how things worked out. Much to Aisha's pleasant surprise, Millie was like a shadow. Although Aisha saw evidence of the other woman's presence in the home, Millie was rarely physically present. The den became a very comfortable media room, thanks to the renter, not that she was ever around to use it. Millie had assignments that kept her away most of the time. One of the signs that she had returned was that the kitchen was stocked with health-nut foods. Organic, was not a common term in Aisha's grocery vocabulary, but she had to admit some the stuff was pretty tasty. Other than that, she felt she had definitely hit the renter lotto. Or so she thought.

Millie started receiving a lot of packages. Not the small As-Seen-On-TV boxes, or the subscription kind of boxes, but huge packages with *fragile* stamped all over them. Aisha did some mild investigating to make sure these boxes would not bring trouble back into her life. Much to her relief, what Millie received was quite benign.

Aisha's fears set aside; she continued the search to find her prize bitch a mate.

* * * *

Despite Aisha's careful planning and caution, she could not keep the lustful eyes of Ulysses from wandering her way. Four months later, on Labor Day weekend, he appeared again. Aisha had decided to take Shell and Doris to the park for some quality time. Even dogs need extra attention. They ran around, chasing balls and barking, and Aisha was so wrapped up in playtime that she didn't notice the watcher on the park bench. Any passerby would not think twice about the watcher. He was nothing out of the ordinary, with his dog sitting beside him as he shelled and ate peanuts. That was the impression an average person might have, but the person approaching him was not average.

"Hey, mind if I take a load off?"

Ulysses turned to the intruder. He had noticed the dude's approach from the other side of the park. The view told him that something was up. This was not an everyday cat. Sure, he was Roca-clad and had the swagger. But his movement was precise. He seemed to have taken a measure of everyone and everything in 100 yards. If Ulysses had to guess, he'D say this guy was military. Ulysses matched him in height, but pound for pound, it was more like Lewis vs. Jones. There was a lightness in his tone. The brevity caused the detective to dismiss him as a threat. With a nod, he gave the newcomer permission to sit.

"Nice weather and view today," the stranger ventured to start a conversation.

Ulysses did not have to turn his head to not that they were both watching women with two dogs. A non-committal, "Hn," to acknowledge the statement.

Ulysses just nodded and kept one eye on Aisha.

"You more interested in the dogs or the woman?" the stranger asked.

Ulysses turned his head slowly. "What's it to you?"

The stranger didn't say anything else. Instead, he rose and approached Aisha. A wary growling blue nose halted his advance. The dog stopped playing to snarl at the intruder approaching from the rear. Aisha turned around to confront the stranger.

Upon making eye contact, Aisha let out an ecstatic shout, "Patches! When did you get back?"

Not forgetting that Doris was ready to go on the defensive, Aisha took a moment to give her a hand signal to stand down. The hound continued to prance about until Doris let out authoritative snot. That promotes hound to lay down too. Aisha allowed the exchange to play out without taking corrective action. Shell was turning out to be more stubborn than she thought he would be. But Doris was exceeding all her expectations. She could be trusted off-leash. But Shell was not completely ready. But it was a free day for them; she had brought them here to play to their heart's content.

Patches drew her in for a hug, as much a greeting, and had been impressed by her training. His cousin had come a long way. He remembered when she was clumsy and unsure. Now her she was with sight trained dog.

"I got in yesterday. And look at you got Doris following hand signals. The Red one still needs work.

"I know; keep in mind he is still a puppy. How you find you find me out here? " she asked.

"Your roommate," he answered with a grin.

She backed out his embrace with a firm look on her face.

"Chill," his and went up defensively. He remembers quickly how she was touchy about her privacy. And if the new roomie was giving out her where about loosely, there would be hell to pay.

He continued the tale cautiously," She did not exactly say you were here. Hell, she gave me the fifth degree before confirming I knew you.

And even then only said you took the dogs out to play, and if was your cousin, I should call you ".

"She let you in?" Aisha asked

"Naw. She wasn't having that".

Aisha nodded her head, approvingly. Millie was turning out to be a decent roommate. It was rule five, with no random people in the house.

"Do you know you have eyes on you?" Patrick asked, concern on his face.

Aisha sighed, yeah: she looked over his shoulder, and to her annoyance, the agent still had his eyes latched on them. "I was looking for a stud for Doris and came out with a tail."

Patches held her at arms' length, a stern look on his face. "I told you to stay out of trouble while I was gone."

Aisha shrugged him off. "It's alright. They got nothing on me. That one's just sniffing."

"You sure?!" He pressed concern on his face.

"Yeah, I'm completely legit. I only deal in puppies. And now you're here; I can show you my new kennel. It's awesome!"

Patches grinned. "Sure thing, Cuz. But first, we need to deal with that guy. It would be best if you invited him to the cookout. I doubt he's on the clock. I didn't notice any other characters on the way in." That comment earned him a punch in the shoulder.

"Are you mad!?" her eyes wide. She thought this last tour had finally sent her cousin off the deep end.

"I'm not crazy, cuz. Besides, it's that, or I deck him for stalking my cousin."

"You wouldn't." she laughed but knowing he would.

"The guy was staring a hole in your ass. Hell, yeah, I'd lay him out. He's staring hard, am I right?"

Patches continued to use his broad shoulders to shield Aisha from view. While they were growing up, he had made sure that she could take of herself when he wasn't around. The problem was that Aisha liked to get in the *midst*, as she put it, and wind up in a whole lot of mess.

Patches would always have her back, but he was not sure if he could bail her out with the feds involved.

Aisha made a show of getting the ball from Doris to restart their fetch game to check on her stalker. It was just as Patches said. U.K. had not taken his eyes off them. She only snorted a confirmation.

"Well?" her cousin asked.

"Well, what?"

"What are you going to do?"

Aisha rolled her eyes. She had done everything she could think to come off the radar for indictment. That meant there was only one thing left to do: stop acting like a suspect and act like an average woman. Leashing her pets, she gave Patch an apathetic look. "I'll deal with it. Don't worry. "

"By the way, your roommate. She cute. Where'd you find her?"

"She's not the type you usually go for."

He shrugged. "People change. What's her name?"

"Millie. I'll formally introduce you two. "she answered. Slightly amazed, he with new interest.

"Let's head out

The quartet filed out of the park without giving Ulysses another look. Aisha loaded her babies into the DeVille. While Patrick revved his Suv's engine waiting for her to get going, She would deal with him later. Aisha truly hoped he would just go away, but someone had once told her once you're on fedar (federal radar), you stay on fedar, maybe for years. She had nothing to hide, but she still didn't want them to follow her everywhere she went. Especially not at the family cookout, the haven where she could relax with her cousins and let the dogs lumber about.

The cookout was great, better than a planned reunion. Patches, Aisha, and some other cousins went off into the woods to have a smoke and mingle. Aisha didn't do much of either. She sat on a fallen tree and stared at *Ulysses's* card and her cell phone. If she contacted him, she could be walking into an elaborate setup. Or she'd have a real stalker on her hands. If she didn't call, she would never know. The smart thing to do would be to leave it alone. The reckless thing to do would be to hit Send.

The smart thing was being pushed aside by the reckless thing. The way he looked at her was not the way cops looked at suspects. By know now, he'd have to realize she was not in *the life* and should have gone after better leads. She ran her business on the referral system. It was too easy to get involved with the wrong crowd.

But trouble had found her anyway.

If she were totally honest with herself, she'd admit to liking it. She liked it. She liked the look of Ulysess too. What was life about if not to take a risk? She hit Send.

The phone rang and rang, and she was about to hang up when the voice mail picked up. That smooth accent touched a sensitive nerve. "Make the message brief," it said. "I am a busy man."

The arrogance, but that's what I like. The beep sounded. "Book a room, someplace nice. I'll meet you there."

When she closed the phone, she found herself in a headlock. "Whacha doing, cuz?"

"Patches, get off me."

"Come on; Uncle Job is telling one his stories. I heard some about cat litter and a hill. It's going to be funny," Patches pulled her off the log and into the family.

Meanwhile, Ulysses was sitting in a sports bar waiting for his contact. Despite the noise from the ballgame, he heard his phone. But he did not answer it, thinking that the recorded message might be more useful. As always, his contact was taking his sweet time. He was prepared to give a haphazard report, receive a reprimand, then be on his way.

Keeping tabs on Aisha was not just recreation. He was certain she was connected, and chances were that she would lead to someone higher up the food chain. And even if she wasn't, he had other prospects. This assignment was going to be his ticket off this joint task force. He looked at his phone to find out who was calling. It was a local number. Even better, it was Miss Harris's number. The call would go unanswered h.

However, he was able to listen to ms. Greene's message before the contact had taken up the seat next to him.

"What's the score, my friend?"

Ulysses did not bother with the usual cryptic talk. He had devised a plan wherein he could have his cake and eat it, too. "You remember that hungry kid, Neal? If we play it right, this one is going to be our golden ticket. One more thing—if that kid is still working security at the Omni, get me a room there, the same night he is on."

"That place is pricey." Groaned the contact.

"Call me when it's set up." Ulysses finished his drink and left the contact sitting at the bar.

Much to the dismay of his current handlers, Ulysses did not believe in timetables. He had gotten this assignment because he understood dogs. When it came to man or beast, he had one philosophy: a lot of time, patience, and work had to be invested before either could be used. Tenure as a detective plus two generations of K-9 unit veterans had taught him that. He had been working on a murder case in Tennessee when the suspects started crossing state lines, and the evidence was leading to other criminals and crimes. The Bureau got involved not long after the first bust. They had their eye on Bartholomew Jackson, also known as Bajah, for many things, including trafficking, illegal gambling, and animal endangerment. It only made sense for them to recruit Ulysses. He was already under, and all he had to do was go a little deeper.

Ulysses had calculated his way through all of Baja's contacts, getting introduced to one middle man after another until he met The Man. All he needed to close the case was to catch Baja in the act of doing anything illegal. His sole miscalculation was meeting Aisha. Her name was not unfamiliar to him. Their local informant, Rodney Watson, had briefly mentioned her. Who turned out to be her former lover. Watson insisted that she had nothing to do with business, but that was before he got busted. Aisha seemed well connected.

He checked on the information he gleaned from the meeting. Aisha's side hustle was technically legit. The law saw people as guilty by association. So because some of her past clients had rap sheets, She was now under scrutiny. According to Bajah, she was worth meeting, even if what she wanted would seem unusual. But Ulysses had taken her too lightly and messed up.

One call is all it took; all the targets had gone ghost. By the time Ulysses put it together what was at the cause, she had covered her tracks too. Only the house was left, with a paper trail leading back to Ms. Elly Watson, the mother of Rodney Watson. On the surface, it looked like Aisha was taking care of her ex-boyfriend's senile mother. Aisha's financial records revealed that she was like many others.

Americans, living above her means and in debt. Ulysses, on the other hand, found Miss. Greene to be calculated and cunning. He and did not believe that the data was telling the whole story. He made it clear to the handlers that if one call was all it took to undo all their hard work, then another call phone might get them back on track. Therefore, he would make it his mission to use his time with Miss Greene more wisely the second time around.

To Aisha's dismay, the weekend ended uneventfully, and by Wednesday, she was pretending that she didn't care if the phone rang or not. She wanted the phone to ring very badly. The waiting only made her angry and more suspicious. Something was not right. What man (federal agent or not) turns down a good lay, especially when she's the lay?

She took an early lunch while nursing coffee in the break, her cell phone rang. Fumbling to get it out of her purse, she was slightly deflated to see it was just a text message. She would have preferred to hear a rich baritone, but all she got was a black and white message. She read the message with a smirk and growing anticipation.

It seemed like an eternity before the week came to an end, and she could get her itch scratched. She was hot and bothered long before she snapped the last clasp of her garter belt on the lacey thigh-high stockings. She gave herself the once-over in the vanity mirror, pleased with the seductive image. A light dusting of makeup enhanced her features. There was no sense in using a lot for it to get smeared everywhere. The 'do' is spiky and sassy, instead of hard spritzed curls. She applied a little more of her *"sugar daddy"* lip gloss. She wanted to look, smell, and taste like candy. Sliding into her four-inch heels and pulling a grey swing coat, she ushered her pups downstairs to their sitter.

Millie looked up from her notebook to acknowledge Aisha as Doris hunkered beneath the writer's feet to coax a belly rub. "Doris, you spoiled Millie, chided she gave in to the dog's request.

To Aisha, she waved good night. "Have fun, hot mama."

Aisha didn't pay the little jab any mind, and she had it all worked out. Happily, she tipped her way to the garage and slid into the DeVille. Turning over the ignition and hitting the lights, she was ready to begin the trek uptown. But before she could crest the portal, a sliver sparkle caught her attention. She sighted the gray finish of the Suzuki 900 propped against the far wall.

"That Millie is always full of surprises," she murmured as she backed out the drive to encounter her thrill ride for the evening.

Forty minutes later, she pulled into the hotel's parking deck. The security guard could barely tell her how to get into the building. He was too busy grinning in her face. But she brushed him off and found her way inside. The lobby was classy, embellished with and gold accents on top of marble flooring. But spending so much for a one-night stand in a place like this seemed a bit much. However, standing in the middle of the floor gaping was killing the high-class hooker look she was going for and replacing it with country bumpkin. *Not cute.* It would have been nice if Ulysses had shown up right then.

Brushing aside any mood-killing thoughts, she strolled toward the reception desk and asked for Mr. Kingsley's room. Despite the clerk's snobby manner, they had a pleasant exchange that gained Aisha an envelope and the room key. She waited until she was alone in the elevator to read her note. Thirty seconds later, she wished she had not bothered to open it. It was an arrogant message from a vain man. If he were anyone else, she would not have come. If she were not caught in the grip of the horrible monster called lust, she would not be half-naked and randy with anticipation. But knowing she was playing with fire was making the experience irresistible. The elevator came to a halt on the twenty-second floor. She found Room 2257. As the plastic card slid into the lock pad, her mind raced. What was she going to find inside?

The suite had a dim glow, but at least it was not black, beige, or gold; she'd seen enough of that in the lobby. The room had a soothing color scheme of royal blue and vanilla blended with the city skyline showing through the windows. A bucket of champagne and chocolate-dipped strawberries were the next items to catch her eye. Tossing her jacket aside, she poured herself a generous glass and indulged in the candied fruit. Lazily scanning the horizon, she soon realized that the room could be easily watched from the office building across the street. Maybe she was paranoid, but it was a logical conclusion. Toying with the blinds, she considered closing them but decided that the idea of having an audience for this little affair would be more fun. She left the blinds alone. If the feds wanted a performance, she would give them one.

Ulysses knew when Aisha entered the hotel. He saw her when she picked up the key. Ulysses had planned it all ahead of time. But he had to make sure that the right people saw her too. Ulysses had contacted Neal early in the week. The kid was suspicious as expected, but Ulysses keeps the dialogue short and to the point. He put the bug in Neal's ear that he may be looking for a buyer soon. But after tonight, the pawn would take the bait and run with it. That left one last task for the night. Miss Harris had essentially served her purpose, and he should walk away. Leaving the building without crossing the line and keeping his professional code of ethics should have been his top priority. But he just couldn't keep himself from making mistakes when it came to that woman. He had watched her walk across the lobby, and he liked the roll-bounce movement of her hips. He rubbed his hand over the beard he had not yet gotten used to, even after months of growing it.

Rubbing his beard had become a sign of his irritation. Indecision was keeping him in that lobby. He could go back to his hideout and let the woman enjoy her champagne alone. But he wanted her, and the feeling was mutual.

He boarded the same elevator that Aisha had ridden. The confined space was still full of the lingering scent of a woman's perfume. Ulysses entertained himself with the thought that it was hers. The smell with thick and sweet without being over-powering; it reminded him of candy. He got off on the twenty-second floor and proceeded to the door that matches the room number. He banished any second thoughts. It was wrong, deliciously wrong. Not wanting to spook his guest, Ulysses opened the door cautiously. He had told his keepers that they did not need to send surveillance. But the damn perverts could not resist the prospect of watching a live porno and set up shop anyway. Ulysses calmly resigned himself to the thought it was his civic duty to enter the overprice hotel room and fuck this woman into submission in the name of justice.

He waited a minute to allow his eyes to adjust to the darkness. The vision before him said nothing was separating him from the prize, even though his instincts were saying something else: *You know she's wearing some lingerie. And it would be best if you, soldier boy, touched every inch of lace, sateen, or silk that covers that very feminine form standing in the window before you rip it off and bend her over.*

The instant his hand touched the rise of her hip, Aisha leaned forward. As their body fit flush together, she gave him a slow and inviting grind.

"You ate all the strawberries," he teased her, tracing her back and shoulders with a finger.

"No, I didn't. I saved you the juiciest one. Are you ready for it?"

Ulysses had every right to have a smug look on his face. His bedmate still lay unconscious, exhausted, and snoring while he had showered and dressed. Only when the smell of fresh coffee filled the air did he notice a change in the sleeping woman. The rustling of sheets was followed by sharp groan, and Aisha's eyes flew open in response to the spasm of her overworked loins. Only able to flop onto her back, Aisha lay staring at the ceiling and collecting her thoughts.

Ulysses took the opportunity to seize and toy with one of her exposed nipples.

"Off!" She pushed him away. "I'm not ready yet." The sight of her discomfort only heightened his machismo. "Too bad. I could go a few more rounds."

Aisha rolled her eyes. "Shut up. I hope your friends enjoyed the show."

"Friends?"

"Whatever. I know what you are," She tried to move, but the large hand on her chest prevented her from getting up.

"Stay," he said. "It'll be a while before housekeeping comes knocking."

"The government must pay well for you to afford to shack up in a place like this." She grinned as she threw out the cynical jab. But Ulysses quickly ended her prickly mood by suckling and licking her lips. "I don't know what you're talking about," he said. "I am just a man with expensive interests." He stood up, pulled his jacket on, and exited the room, leaving Aisha alone to deal with her aches and rekindled desire.

When Ulysses reached the lobby, his phone rang. The keepers were checking in. The plan was working. Neal had been standing behind the desk when Aisha arrived. The plan was working out just like Ulysses said it would. He could consider his romp with the breeder his reward. He had his in with the kid. Aisha was right about him, but was not going to confirm the accusation.

Secret Lives

When Aisha came in from walking Shell and Doris, she was surprised to see her tenant in the living room, watching television.

"Hey!" she said, "I thought you were in Rio or something."

Millie waited for the woman and dogs to enter the room before replying. "No. I went to Roanoke to see the leaves change. It's beautiful this time of year."

Shell charged across the room to get petted as Millie idly flipped through the channels.

"Only you would drive through hick land," Aisha said.

"It's not that bad. Your cousin rode is his bike up with me. He's good company. How do you feel about a movie night? I know it's against your code and everything, but I'd appreciate the company."

"It's not a code," Aisha said. "It's just good business sense. You don't have to be friends with the landlady. I haven't eaten yet. Do you feel like Chinese or pizza?"

Aisha was purposefully avoiding making any comment about Patches and Millie getting. If things went bad she did not want to get caught in the middle.

"Landlady? I prefer to think of you as my neighbor. Pizza sounds good. I'll call the pizzeria."

When the pizza was on its way, Aisha opened the entertainment unit and pulled a few DVDs out of their hodgepodge collection. Aisha called out a few titles and they settle on the odd lineup of Casablanca, *The Fences*, and Scarface.

"We should have a beer," Millie muttered, heading to the kitchen. By the time, she returned the first movie had started. She gave Aisha a bottle of *Michelob*. "I'm going on a long trip, coming up," she said.

"That's nothing new. What has you in a funk?"

"My family wants me to come home for the holidays, and I don't want to go to."

Aisha gave her pointed look "You would rather go to the middle of nowhere than see your family?"

Millie nodded her head. "Why?"

"You don't know my family. They're gonna ask a bunch of unnecessary questions, like, Why aren't you married? Are you going to a good church? Not one of those TV charlatans, I hope? Why did you give up your position and condo in exchange for a roommate and a job that has you gallivanting about like a hobo?"

Aisha couldn't help but laugh. "Sorry," she said. "Sorry. But doesn't every family ask those questions? Just give them some generic answers and move on."

"It's not that easy," Millie said. "I have two brothers ... and then there's the feud.... It's like we're some Technicolor version of *Dynasty*. 'Aunt Jessie, she thinks she knows everything. My mom calls her the lying heifer.' And says, 'you know how your cousins are, we cannot have them over.' My Grandfather gets meaner every year, so you have to watch what you say or he might shot. He keeps a rifle around in case the Sheets show up." Both women were laughing by now."

"And," Millie continued, "'will someone make sure Ida took her meds and keep Calvin out the liquor?' They were grooming him for politics until the accident. And here's my favorite. 'Howard (my brother the lawyer), tell us about all the important people you know.' What makes it worse is that my brother the lawyer married the mayor's daughter, the silly Barbie Doll that she is. It never ends. They're a bunch of snobs just because they own over a quarter of the land in that backwater town and the church was built by our maternal great great grandmother's second husband. And the only reason my dad's family owns the land is because great Uncle Roscoe Johnson blackmailed the sheriff. If it wasn't for the pulled pork and collard greens," she finished, "I wouldn't even consider going."

Aisha laughed herself into a bellyache. "That … that is… Wow… I have never heard you talk so much. Or sound so hostile."

"It's not funny! And to make matters worse, I'd have to deal with them on top of jet-lag."

"Millie, that's what trips me out about you. You're willing to go to the far ends of the earth for your company, but you won't drive six hours to visit your family. Just put on that dusty Casablanca coat of yours and go see your people!" Aisha finished her statement with a deep swig of beer to cool her throat.

"Why don't you come with me?" Millie asked. "There are a lot of natural tourist attractions there."

"You are not going to con me into visiting your people, and sightseeing isn't my thing. Besides, I have enough troubles with my own family."

Millie raised an eyebrow. "Do you? You don't talk about 'em." The beer was starting to get to her, and she was only able to focus on Aisha's busy hands. She watched as Aisha pulled a wooden box out under the couch. And out of the box came a small plastic baggie full of leaves, a box of rolling papers, matches, and a plastic container. Aisha twisted the container in half, and then carefully poured a portion of the green leaves and seeds into the bottom.

"What is that for?" Millie asked.

"This is a grinder. It crushes the seeds and makes the leaves finer for a smoother smoke." Aisha held up the cap up so Millie could see the plastic blades inside it. Then she demonstrated how the tool worked, twisting the two halves together, and grating the leaves and seeds into a fine mulch. She emptied the flakes onto a paper, made a fold and glided the long side along her tongue to seal the paper. Then using friction created by her hand on her thigh to roll it up in one quick motion. To Millie, it looked like poetry in motion, a skilled trick learned from years of practice. But when her landlady offered her the first puff she had to turn it down.

"A contact is good enough for me."

"More for me, then," Aisha said. "I don't talk about my family 'cause they're just my family. Mom, my aunts and uncles, my brother, we just share the same blood.

That's all we have in common. Only my cousin Patches and I are tight. Now that he's in the Marines, I don't get to see him that much."

Millie opened another beer. "Patches?"

"Don't tell me you been up North so long you forgot how we name our chaps in the dirty South"

"My family is uppity. Did you forget?"

"I gotcha. We were always in the midst as kids. But we grew up, got a little smarter. Patches … you can call him Patrick, he's a career Marine. He has been in for almost ten years now, Whoa Core and all that mess." She leaned back against the cushions, enjoying the inhale.

"Your family sounds normal to me."

"That's why I picked you, ya know. If it doesn't affect your little world, you don't care. We've been living in the same house for like the burning hour now, and this is the first time either of us has said more than hello and goodbye."

"I thought you wanted it that way."

"I'm not complaining. But haven't you ever wondered why I got a roommate?"

Millie sipped her beer, staring at the floor. Aisha's sudden interest in their living arrangement perplexed her. It had been only by chance that she had found out about Aisha's basement suite. An acquaintance of an acquaintance of Millie's secretary knows Aisha. It always amazed Millie how people affected each others' lives without knowing it. But why she was currently in Aisha's life she did not know, nor had she taken the time to examine this topic.

"No," she finally said. "Not really."

Taking another puff, Aisha gave Millie a weighty look. "Tell me why you're putting together a gallery in my basement, and I'll tell you why I needed a roommate like you."

"Why does it matter all of a sudden?" "Beer and herb make me chatty."

Millie settled back and tried not to laugh at Aisha drug-induced commentary on the film they were sort of watching. When the door bell rang, Aisha jumped up, fumbling for money to pay the pizza boy. The bitter- sweet smell of the herb must have been strong, because the minute she made eye contact with him, he gave her a knowing wink and headed back to his tricked out Supra. When she returned to the den, only her two spoiled dogs where waiting. She gave the pair a treat of meat and cheese from the box before sentencing them upstairs for the night.

"Millie?" she called. When there was no answer, she assumed that her roommate had gone to the bathroom and resumed her smoking and drinking.

"You might understand if I show you." Millie's voice came from behind the sofa. She had come back into the room so quietly that Aisha hadn't noticed.

Aisha looked around, but Millie was already heading back to her part of the house. Bitten by the curiosity bug, Aisha followed her down the kitchen stairs to Millie's mini-storehouse of books, memorabilia, and art. The tour came to a stop in Millie's bedroom. At first, Aisha didn't get it. What she saw was just a portrait of a girl in a sheer white sundress, the shade and light of the paint revealing her form beneath the fabric. The girl was standing in a hallway, looking at some unseen object, perhaps a mirror. At first glance the pretty face in the picture looked sure and confident, but the eyes were innocent and amazed by what they were seeing. The girl was leaning away from the thing she encountered, betraying apprehension or fear. Overall, the painting revealed vulnerability. Aisha was taken aback by the sudden sense that she was spying on this girl, catching her in a moment confusion or uncertainty. It was a beautiful piece, in which the muted colors expressed a multitude of meanings and implications.

"So," Aisha finally said, "you like this person's work and buy the reproductions?"

"Most of these are Taylar's originals. The prints belong to random artists who remind me of Taylar. I gave up everything to find the one who painted my portrait," Millie confessed with mild embarrassment.

"Are you in love with this person, or something?"

"I don't know. I don't think so. How I feel about Taylar isn't easy to describe. Anyway it's your turn."

"I am sleeping with a federal agent who wants me to roll on the dog men."

Millie had not expected anything legally incriminating to fall out of Aisha's mouth. After a minute, she said, "He must not come with benefits if you need a roommate."

"I never thought I'd tell anyone what I was doing on the side, and that's all you have to say?"

"It's not my business. If someone asks me, all I can say is that Aisha is my landlady. We don't go any deeper than that." Millie gave a wink and a smile. A minute later, wanting to steer the conversation away from anything that might land them in the state penitentiary, she said, "So tell me, why is your cousin's name Patches?"

"I couldn't say Patrick when we were kids," Aisha explained, comforted by the thought that Millie's change of topic was a hint that she understood.

The next week could not have been better, for Aisha. Monday afternoon, an associate contacted Aisha about a dog that had been abandoned, one that exhibited all the key features she was looking for in a mate for Doris. After work, she high-tailed it to the country to have a look at this wonder dog. He was everything she had dreamed off, the perfect mate for her precious Doris, at least on the out side. She contacted her veterinarian the next morning to have the blood work done. His temperament was not exactly what she wanted, but it would do if the genetics matched up, the litter would be physically amazing. Al- though she truly believed in the genetic vigor of hybrids, she was painfully away that not every hybrid was equal. That's why a standard, with specific bred characteristics and lineage are necessities for man's best friend. Aisha be- lieved she was on the verge of creating something lasting. It all started with Max and Megan, how she loved them. Megan was beautiful, blue grey, obedient and protective Cane corso. Max was a blue nose pit and a lilac Sharpei, a loyal laid back kind of dog.

Aisha loved their huge heads and strong bodies. She thought of them as perfect in every way. Max ironically was a gift from Rodney. Mad was supposed to be breed from fierce fight dogs. But he came out the runt of the litter and lacking aggressive tendencies. Rodney's friends were going cull him or worse. But, the Fates were not on Max's side, a copperhead snake ended his life. That dog was the only good gift Rodney gave her, that, and a surrogate mother.

She was so excited she could hardly focus on her work. When she looked at the calendar on her desk, the date brought her back to earth, a little calmer, but still happy. It was hump day and the weekend was coming up fast, which meant that she and Ms. Elly would make their weekly visit to the farmers market. Despite all the other memories that Alzheimer's had taken from Ms. Elly, it had not disturbed her memory of the open markets. Before old age had set in Elly and her husband had farmed the land behind their house. Every fall they would take the harvest to the farmers market. Aisha re- membered Rodney talking about the trips, with disgust. He hated it. But Aisha was all city-girl and she loved the novelty of it.

Saturday came and just as Aisha thought, Ms. Elly remembered that the girl in the champagne car was coming to take her to the market. The nurse waiting with her had had an ear full of about the market, and was ready to hand over her charge as soon as Aisha walked in. Ms. Elly was cute in her favorite red coat and plaid wool skirt. It remembered Aisha of their time together in years past. It reminded Aisha of their time together in years past.

Delivery

Shirley Jones was good for showing up at worst times. It did not matter if she telephoned ahead or suddenly appeared; it was always a bad time for Aisah. This Saturday afternoon was no different, except Shirley surprised Aisha by not nagging her about how she lived. Instead, she initiated a spring cleaning campaign. To add to the unexpected, Ms. Shirley declared they should have Sunday dinner together before leaving. Any other time the proclamation would have lead to an argument, but time Aisha agreement without protest.

    The encounter left Aisha unnerved. They never got along. They had not been able to share the same space without arguing since Aisha was ten. Something was going to go wrong. An ill wind was headed her way. She could feel it. But she still had things to do.

    She was so caught up in the hum of the vacuum that she almost didn't hear the doorbell ring. When she opened the door, she saw an unknown man on her front porch.

    "Aisha Greene?" as the man in the Polo shirt and khakis.

    "Who's asking?"

    The man handed her a legal-sized envelope. Aisha's toes went cold at the sight of it. She had seen that kind of legal document at a law firm she had once worked for temporarily.

    "Ms. Greene, you have been subpoenaed."

It would have been better if the ground had opened and swallowed her whole, instead of having to hear those words. Subpoena equaled every negative thing her mother had ever said to her. The backlash hit her like a wave. She was not the only one who would be affected if she had to go up the river. What about Miss Elly? Who would sit with her on Sunday afternoons and read the paper? Or take her to the farmers market? Who could take in Doris and shell? These thoughts and fears raced through Aisha's mind. It wasn't just a court summons; it was more like a death sentence.

Once the envelope rested in Aisha's hands, the courier walked back to his vehicle, turning a deaf ear to the flow of profanity that spilled from Aisha's mouth. She might look like a lady, but at that moment, she sounded like a sailor. She closed the door and pounded into the kitchen, hunting the cabinets for the hidden bottle of *Patron reserve*. Seated at the kitchen table, she went over the events of the last year—the choices she had made, the actions she had taken. It all came to one conclusion; she hadn't done enough. Millie was right. Her friend did not come with benefits. But she hadn't expected any favors, just a good lay. Her first and third shot came and went before she was able to open the envelope. It took two more before she was able to read the document inside. It was worse than she had expected. To be indicted was one thing, but to be called as a witness was another.

Ratting even the lowest cronies was not a good idea. Besides, it was beneath her. They were all hustlers, angling to get ahead and stay out of each others' way. As she continued to drink, questions arose in her head. How the hell did she get on fedar? And why would she be so damn important? Simple. She knew all those jokers.

She didn't hear Millie drive into the garage. She didn't hear the basement door open, or Millie was calling out to see if she was home.

"Aisha! Doris! Shell?" Neither dog nor human answered her call. The house was dark, and the vacuum cleaning was sitting in the middle of the living room floor.

Millie looked out the patio door. The dogs were locked in their kennel. The Cadillac was parked. Aisha had to be home. Something wasn't right. Millie was about to go searching through the house when she heard a sob from the kitchen. Turning cautiously, Millie spotted Aisha, her head bowed over a shot glass full of tequila.

Aisha groaned as Millie got her back up into a sitting position. As her eyes adjusted to the light, she almost cried. "Oh, Miss Celie, I's goin' ta jail." Aisha downed the shot then poured herself another shot.

Millie was stupefied. She knew it had to bad if Aisha was talking like she was in, *The Color Purple*. As Aisha brought the drink to her lips, Millie noticed the letter under her arm." What is this?" Millie retrieved the document and began to examine it. Aisha poured another shot. It was not as bad as she thought. The word indictment did not appear anywhere on the page. But to be called to the witness stand was probably just as bad for Aisha. Millie sat beside Aisha and tried to take the tequila away.

"What I's gon' do?" Aisha moaned.

"Aisha, listen to me." Millie wasn't sure what to say at first, but then the words started coming out. "You cannot perjure yourself, nor can you talk about what these fools do in their spare time. Remember, you are just a witness, so you only have to attest to what you have seen. Everything else you think you know or have heard is hearsay. Testimony like that will just get you and others in trouble."

"Huh?"

"What? Just because I read all day doesn't mean I read junk. Some of my clients are legal eagles. Come on. Get up. Your date with José is over."

"It's *Patron*."

"Whoever, let's go. I'll bring the children in later."

* * * *

A month later, the court date arrived, and Aisha was without her preferred support. Patches was on back on base and unavailable for her to lean on. In preparation for the day, Aisha had been doing some soul searching and reconciling. Reflecting on the past few days, she could not shake the feeling that she would be getting bad news, no matter what happened on the stand. Shell and Doris were put into Mr. Dawkins's care, with instructions if she didn't come back. She had to be ready for anything. She also left Millie instructions about the house and how to carry out Ms. Elly's living will if she was indicted and sentenced after her testimony.

The courthouse was a domineering gray building. Aisha prayed for strength as she proceeded inside. The institution's speckled vinyl floor gleamed beneath the fluorescent lights. Despite the brightness, Aisha struggled to find the light at the end of the tunnel. After joining the herd of people being funneled through the security point, she looked around for the bailiff. When she found one, he escorted her into the waiting room until her turn to take her stand. Time passed slowly in the little room. She wanted something to drink, but she wasn't allowed outside, and all she had seen on the way in was a fountain in the hall. Sneaking out for a quick sip had crossed her mind a half dozen times before the clock said she had been there ten minutes.

The hours crawled by before the bailiff returned to take her into the courtroom.

She finally got her sip of water, but it didn't help. The doors opened. Aisha felt immediately attacked. The glare of high-voltage lights on mahogany was jarring after having been a less illuminated space. She took a step back, but the hand on her shoulder urged her forward. Using the witness stand as a focal, she thought of it as a magnet drawing her in. Sworn in, she took her seat. She surveyed the room before the attorney began. That was enough time to identify half a dozen faces she wished she could erase from her memory. It was too late for that. They were all going down. She and Baja made eye contact, and his characteristic golden grin guided her line of sight to a sick-looking inmate being escorted out. The man leaving the room was her Ex. Baja mouthed to her, "You're straight," and turned back around to converse with his lawyer. No else seemed to notice this little exchange.

Why was Rodney here? I don't know what this about. I just wanted to breed does. Why? Had the feds offered him a deal? She held on to what Ms. Shirley and Millie had said: give straight answers, no more, no less. The lawyer began, he asked her to state her full name, and it went downhill from there.

"Do you recognize the defendants, Miss Greene?"

"Yes."

"Where have you seen them?"

"At parties."

"What kind of parties?"

"A party. A gathering of friends and associates," she replied defensively.

"We are all acquainted with the definition. What we want to know is what kind of activities took place at these parties."

Aisha tensed up before answering. "Dancing, card playing, drinking...."

The lawyer cut off her vague answer with another question, "Were there dog fights, Miss Greene?"

"Yes. Sometimes, dogs are like people. They don't always get along."

"Were Mr. Bartholomew Jackson, also know as Bajah, and his co-defendants' promoters of these events, where dogs don't get along?".

'I've known Mr. Jackson to host a variety of private events." She mentally kicked herself for saying too much.

"Private events, you say. Then is it to be our understanding that these parties were by invitation only? You are an accountant and financial advisor. Is that correct? Thus, the court can assume you are associated with him on that level, as well? Why else would you be invited to VIP events unless you are providing him with your services?"

"Wait a minute!" She burst out at the same time the defense objected.

The judge struck the gavel and gave the prosecutor a warning before instructing Aisha to answer the first question. She was fuming, but she answered in the most level tone she could achieve.

"Yes, I am a CPA. No, I don't know what Baj—Mr. Jackson's actual profession is, and I don't handle his accounting. I know some of the co-defendants because we went to high school together. The others lived in the old neighborhood. But I don't hang out with them on a regular basis. The only reason I am acquainted with Mr. Jackson is because of a mutual associate. Does that answer all of your questions, Mr. Prosecutor?"

The attorney took his time to respond, picking out another question from his notes.

"Would you please tell the court the name of the person that introduced you to Mr. Jackson?"

"Rodney Watson," she replied without hesitation." How do you know, Mr. Watson, Miss Greene?"

"We were lovers."

Aisha had no moral qualms about implicating Rodney. And it was a complete lie. So the prosecution wanted her to drop a name he would be the first choice every day. He hadn't to write or call home in over a year. Poor Ms. Elly was always asking about him. All she could do was deflect, distract, or reassuring her that her son was Ok.

The lawyer spoke again. "Ah, I see. My sources tell me that you are handling Mrs. Watson's finances. She is currently in a nursing home, correct?"

"Yes. Rolling Green."

"That's an expensive facility. And it seems you are living in the home Of Mrs. Watson. You are also taking care of her expenses at Rolling Green Nursing home. It must be difficult. How have you been able to pay for it? Even on your salary, it must be a strain. Perhaps you have a part-time position? Or are you into something riskier? Like breeding dogs for fighting"."

The defense spoke up. "You're Honor, I object. The witness is not on trial. Miss. Greene is doing a noble thing, taking care of her former lover's ailing mother."

The defense was definitely pulling double duty, trying to keep Baja out of jail and keeping the prosecution off Aisha.

The judge agreed, and the prosecutor had to back down.

"Your Honor, I would like to address his accusation." Aisha was furious. She hated the stigma attached to the dog she bred.

"If you wish," the judge granted her request.

Aisha didn't miss the levity in the judge's tone. It seemed as he was eager for her to say things inflammatory in her aggravated state. Looking out across the room, she saw the defender was shaking his head. Aisha was determined to have her say.

"What you really want to know is if I can be another target for an Animal cruelty witch hunt. What I am, sir, is a hybrid enthusiast. My dogs are well cared for and loved. I breed dogs that are intelligent and trainable. I do sell many of my pups. I do everything to code. But I can't control what happens to those little lives when they leave me.

Ordinary people like strong dogs. I provide that. It is not a crime to do so. I am to afford my lifestyle and take of Ms. Elly because I understand how to manage money. That is not a crime either." She ended her speech with a glare in the prosecutor's direction.

"Your honor, I think we can move on," the defense added quickly. Leaving both the judge and prosecutor miffed that they were going to get anyone else today.

Aisha's time on the stand concluded with her being asked to point to any one in the room she had seen at one of Baja's events. Then she was told she could exit the stand. She was led to another room. A man in a dark suit was waiting for her there.

"Who are you?" she asked.

"I had considered that you wouldn't recognize me."

Ulysses had cut the dreads and goatee and lost the accent. she said. "Shouldn't you be on another assignment by now?"

"Maybe. I just wanted to say that I'm not the one who put you up there. And that that Rodney kid wants to talk to you."

The door behind Ulysses opened, and the chained jumpsuit from the courtroom walked in.

Aisha looked Rodney up and down, rolling her eyes. "Don't be that way, Aisha," he said. "I want to thank you for taking care of my mom...."

"Whatever, you snitch."

"Listen, I know you been getting my letters. Have you been reading them to Ma?"

She continued to glare at him.

"This one may be my last one. "

"What bullshit are you talking about? They don't give snitches the chair."

"Naw. It ain't like that. I'm sick. See, I got cancer, and it's spreading fast. I don't know how much time I have. So when DA approached me, I just told them what I knew. I didn't find out till after the investigation started that you were partying with some of my old friends. Sheltered like you are, you don't know this, but a lot of them are grimy. So please, just be good." he pleased with her.

Aisha listened carefully to the words Rodney was choosing. The feds were still listening, and he was trying to protect her. They were all trying to protect her, Patches, Ulysses, Bajah, and Rodney. Was she that much of a troublemaker? It was utter insanity.

"Don't worry about I just want to make sure Ms, Elly is taken care of," she replied. "She was always sweet to me. She is in Rolling Greene assisted living. I take her to the flea market on the weekends. You should call my old number on Saturday morning, so you two can talk. If you can?"

Ulysses coughed to get their attention. "Time to go, Watson. Miss. Greene, I'll be seeing you."

Aisha watched the guards lead Rodney out of the tiny room, unsure whether she felt sad, glad, or angry. Baja had given her a pass, so there would be no repercussions at home. Rodney was dying and trying to make his peace. Ulysses was making plans to linger in her life. And Patches was probably going to run off with her roommate. Her life had gotten too complicated.

Another bailiff escorted her out of the room and said that she was free to go. Sweeter words had never been spoken.

The Exciting Life

There is a good reason they call the weather change of the Pacific Ocean El Niño. It kicks and howls, just like the little boy in seat 9F. However, neither the turbulence in the jet stream nor the screaming child inside could disturb the sense of euphoria that enveloped one of the jet's passengers. This elated feeling was a welcomed change after a tension filled week. At the last minute, Millie had been asked to represent Funderburke Press at a conference in California. Unfortunately, she was so concerned about her landlady's well-being that she could hardly focus on the workshop. Thankfully, none of her colleagues seemed to notice her lack of interest.

On the last day of the conference, Millie got a phone call from Aisha to know that everything had worked out. There was no need for her to rush home. Millie shouted hallelujah the moment she hung up. Which caused some of the people around her to take extra interest in her. But Millie did not care, she was relieved, and the only thing she wanted right now was a vacation. Standing at the American airline check-in desk of LAX, she exchanged her ticket to North Carolina for one to Belize. The name screamed, Vacation.

It started raining the moment she landed. All she could do was laugh; rain was her good omen. An ironic running theme since she started traveling, she had the best experiences when it rained. She enjoyed every minute in Belize, even in the face of a tropical storm.

Unlike the other tourists, who had consigned themselves to hotel rooms, Millie found a local watering hole. She spent the entire weekend dancing with the natives.

The night before her excursion ended, the storm moved on. Once the roads and landing strip dried out, the jet could take off without a hitch into beautiful azure skies. Gazing down at the vanishing land below, Millie seriously started to consider a retirement plan to Belize. To live somewhere where the people care and actively protected their ecosystem, and are genuinely nice, is extremely attractive. But retirement is a long way off and Millie needed to get her head back in work mode. During the no electronics period, she mediates, putting her thoughts in order,

When the light does go off, she reluctantly pulls the smartphone from her purse. Millie preferred to keep *The Thing*, as she liked to call it, turned off if possible. She hadn't looked at it once in three days; there wasn't a need to. She had contacted Thomas and the office before she left California. Thomas was happy with her report. The office had new reviews and technical advice to mull over, everyone was happy. The screen of her inbox indicated that it was full. No surprise there. She liked the feeling of being inaccessible in a downloadable world.

I have this phone-PC to do my job and have an overpowered dirt bike to make my life easier, but I don't need them. *Besides, people just don't seem to realize how* disconnected they are from each other with all the techno junk in the way. Texting, e-mail, voice mail, it's all so impersonal these days. Traffic is the only time most people are forced to be conscious of the people around them. No wonder there are so many road rage incidents. It's the consequences of the world we live in.

Thinking about this reminded her that she still had not thanked Deshawn for convincing her to take a computer class. Otherwise, she and *the thing* would not have a working relationship. Opening her inbox, she skimmed over the alerts and reviewed messages until she came across an address he had not seen in a while.

Hey Millie,

Long time, no see. Tanya misses you and wants me to tell you that she is going back to school to become a social worker. Funderburke is finally putting me in the sales and marketing division. He says I'm too people-orientated to be kept in the editing department.

Charlene is beginning to act normal. Thanks to Tanya. Who, Somehow located her daughter and has gotten them to reconcile.

One more thing, Charlene knows a close friend of your painter and has given out your contact info. I know, a complete breach of PI. But who can stop that woman?

Now for the most important news, you need to come back here the first week in October. My African Queen is going to marry me.

Call us
Deshawn Clemons

Millie closed the window and steeled their heart against the unattainable possibility. The odds were too slim that Taylar would come back into her life like a welcomed spring breeze. But she cherished the possibility like an unvoiced wish.

She had started this journey find to find out if she could be the woman in the mirror. She took the risk of turning her life upside down because of a portrait. It had taken some time and a few sleepless, but she overcame many of her personal barriers. Now she only had two fears left. The first was she had not grown. The second was that Taylar would scuff at all her efforts should they meet again. It was too much to think about. Instead, she focused on work and making her way home.

She landed at Charlotte Douglas airport without any problems or delays. It seemed odd. The speed at which she had traveled invoked the feeling that fate was rushing her home. Even the cabbie seemed to be flying through the city. Perhaps it was all the good news she had received on the way back or the end of a wonderful three-day weekend. She had been traveling steadily for over a year as a literary consultant.

The job was not what she had expected. She had to edit all the incoming articles in between, putting conferences and seminars. Her life now could not compare to the one she left behind. Her views on church attendance had undertaken a radical change. Millie had become spiritual, focusing more on using her bible and her prayer mat than sitting in a pew. The whirlwind lifestyle was tiring at times, but Millie would not trade it.

The cab pulled up to the split level house, and she rolled her suitcase up the front steps; the door flew open. Apparently, Millie was not moving fast enough because Aisha had pulled her into the foyer before she could say hello.

"You have a visitor in your room." The way she said it unnerved Millie. She was preparing her mouth to ask who was visiting, but Aisha cut her off. "I know agreed that know Randos in the house. But that person is indescribable."

It took every ounce of will power to keep Millie from running downstairs. Still, nothing could stop her from becoming watery-eyed as she made her way into the lower level. The mounting fear that gripped her chest made her stop and breathe. What if whoever was waiting for her was not that person? She would look so foolish. But what if it was that person? What should she say? She kept walking. She took another deep breath.

Taylar had settled into her favorite chair in a cozy corner constructed out of bookcases and hanging art. Every light seemed to burn ultra-bright, making it easier for Millie to admire the dark head of hair bowed over a book. She stood still as a statue, watching the scene unfold. Taylar didn't seem to notice her. She should just say 'hello' or 'long time no see.' However, all those conventional greetings just seemed unbefitting. Without warning, Taylar flipped to a dog-eared page and began to read aloud:

When I look into the mirror, I want it to crack. I want it to fall and shatter into a million pieces to pierce my bare feet. When I look into the mirror, I see all the horrors in the world. I see what trying to hide from them has made. When I look into the mirror, I feel cold and bitter. I feel as if I should turn my head and pretend it isn't there. When I look into the mirror, I think hardships and simple pleasures make the world worthwhile. I think sometimes it is all too much. When I look into the mirror, I wonder how I fit into this tangled web of life. How do any of us? When I look in the mirror, I hope that our knowledge and technology don't get the better of us. I hope the world turns out the way that dreamers dream. When I look in the mirror, I wish for things I deem unworthy and impossible. I wish…. I don't know what I wish.

By the time Taylar finished reading the passage, Millie had moved to the ottoman in front of the chair. Setting the book aside, the artist pinned her in place with a warm gaze.

"I hope you don't mind," Taylar said. "I didn't realize it was a journal till I was a few pages in."

"it's alright, only because it's you." She was suddenly twenty-six again and smitten by those chocolate almond eyes.

"I heard you were looking for me. Since I was passing thru, I thought I'd stop by. Tell me, what made you write such melancholy prose?"

"I wrote it after I studied the portrait you sent me."

Her response caused Taylar to shift uneasily in the oversized chair. "I barely remember painting it. I found it while I was cleaning out my friend's attic. It took me an entire summer to remember you. I thought you should have it."

Someone who didn't know Taylar would have been hurt. "It was months before I opened the package," she said, "and after that, my life changed. But I don't think I was looking for you. I was looking for myself."

"What did you find?"

"I found that the world can be explored by anyone willing to step outside their box. Taylar, what is your favorite color?"

"Black. Why?"

"I can spot your work in a dark, crowded novelty shop in Vancouver, but I don't know anything about you."

Taylar gave her a smile. " What else do you want to know?"

"Why did you leave the Savannah project? She asked, easing on the bed adjacent to the chair.

Taylar paused, recalling those days.

"You mean the traveling circus? I'm sorry. The revolutionaries were boring. Besides, I found my biological mother and decided to hop on a plane to go meet her. My friend, let me tell you, after meeting her and hearing her story, I understand why she dropped me into the hands of the Niancas. They are the people that raised me. I still can't believe they are truly related to me; they're my second cousins, actually. Not that it makes me like them any better. But a lot of anger was washed away over a cup of coffee with her. I drop by her place ever so often."

Millie was mesmerized and elated. Taylar hadn't said anything profound or inspiring, but the air around them had changed. It was alive and tangible. It smelled like amber and sage. But most importantly, Taylar had caller her friend. They were connecting. Moving beyond just the point of muse and artist.

"I don't remember you being so talkative," she said, trying to grin.

"And I don't remember you being so open-minded." Taylar countered.

"Then I guess we've both changed."

Taylar smiled. "Do you drink coffee? Let me make a pot for you, the Mexican way, or so I'm told. Ground coffee mixed with cinnamon as its percolates. Is your coffee maker in this cabinet?"

Millie nodded and let Taylar search her makeshift kitchenette and make coffee. As the coffee maker on the baker's rack, she asked,

"Taylar, why did you paint me?"

The artist did not answer her at first but filled the pot with water from a 3-gallon container on a baker's rack. Then located cinnamon and coffee (Cinnamon, thanks to Millie's hobby of making herbal tea). Once the pot began to drip, Taylar returned to the chair. She waited patiently for the contemplative look on her new friend's face to vanish.

"Good question," the artist replied in a reflective tone.

"I guess it was because I couldn't get the image of you out of my head. I saw you before we were introduced. You had just entered the gallery. The seconds between you crossing the threshold and viewing the first piece ... the look in your eyes. It was like you wanted everything in the room. The was excitement and thirst in you I found intriguing.—I don't know if anyone else noticed or that you even knew you could look that way. The look in your eyes, I wanted to know if I had the skill to capture that look. I had to preserve the moment. Especially since by the time we were introduced, you had become so mundane.

The coffee was brewed, and Millie filled their cups. "Tell me," she said, "how you did it? how you can with the idea to paint it the way you did."

They talked for hours about painting techniques, work projects, people, places, and things. Taylar revealed one layer after another of the personal information that Millie drank in happily. This went on long into the night, but Millie noticed that Taylar was beginning to disconnect when the conversation began to thin. However, she was not ready to let go. A quiet invitation to stay the night was followed by a convenient excuse that it was too late to wake someone else up or travel again swayed her guest. Taylar sat stark still eyeing the duffel.

"I'll stay if you're okay with sharing the bed. I'm too old to sleep on floors and couches".

With a hearty laugh, Millie agreed to share the bed.

The night was not supposed to end this way. It was not supposed to end with me lying curled next to Millie. I'm not supposed to be dreaming blissfully, holding hands, not wanting to leave. This was not on the program. But somehow, it's alright to be here with her and feel this connected to someone. Even with Kayla and Ulysses, it wasn't like this. But what does that really mean, connected? What do I do with a Muse that has become a friend?

Millie was like twining ivy in Taylar's mind, bringing together abstract thoughts and colors, forming elaborate tapestries that needed to be brought to life. The person, who had been an idle thought, was so inspiring in the flesh. As they slept, their hands had interlocked like two creeper plants tangled in a tropical canopy. Two entities combined, yet independent, growing into and around each other until one snaps to branch off in another direction.

She had asked many questions about Taylar's past, about the comings and goings of people and places. Who was important, and why. But she didn't ask the one question, must people asked or assumed quickly. She just accepted, accepted Taylar, wholly just like Kayla. She often said: It doesn't matter if you wear a dress or suit in this world as long you remember that The Man Upstairs is in charge, and stick to the golden rule. After that, everything else is a cakewalk. At least that was her fall back when psychiatry failed in their debates.

It was one of the many pearls of wisdom written in Taylar's notebook. A book just like Millie's, it was that proof a life experienced. Carefully, quietly Taylar pulled away to study Millie's journal again. Her journal was an unpretentious account of a woman exploring herself and the world around her. There was no logical reason to take Millie's journal. Except that the artist wanted a keepsake from this particular muse. But taking it would be rude, and ripping out a few pages would be worse. The pale light coming in from the windows announced the coming of dawn. It was time to go.

Millie knew the moment Taylar pulled away. Watching through half-open eyes, she saw Taylar take her journal. She didn't say anything until Taylar pulled on an old denim jacket.

"Is it that time already?" she asked from the bed, untangling herself from the sheets.

"I didn't mean to wake you, but I have to catch a train. There is a project I'm working on in New York. When it's done, I'll try to come back here."

Millie felt warm at the prospect of another moment like this. But quickly shoved that thought away. Abruptly she crossed the room.

"Taylar, if you have to go, it's okay. You don't owe me anything, not even an empty promise that you'll come back. The fact that you came means the world to me."

Millie was stunned by her own frankness. Millie knew that not so long ago, she would have asked for a reliable means of communication. Anything to stay in contact But, not now, there was no need to lean on others to experience life. She has so many answers last night that her head was still spinning. She accepted the o

Unable to communicate verbally, Taylar embraced her, glad to know another free spirit, and after a long pause, said," I think I love you.

Millie felt emotionally juvenile in her mental quest for something to say. "I can be your muse phila and agape."

"That's poetic" there was laughter in the artist's voice.

She Could try to hold on to these fleeting moments or choose to let go. Holding on would smoother Taylar, and the artist would rage against her. She got that insight from their talk. The right thing to do would be to let go and preserve the memory.

"Can I take you to the airport?"

"I would like that."

She drove back to the townhouse with a smile on her face, feeling free and inspired. Upon entering her basement suite, she began evaluating the items that she felt defined her life. But nothing stood out. Nothing seemed to embody what was truly important. Her eyes ventured to the portrait that had started her journey, but the emotions it once inspired did so no more. And what did that mean for Millie? Several things, one that she accomplished her goals. Second, it meant that she did not need things to define who she was. Touching the bed and shaking off the euphoria that she had lain there with Taylar, she knew she was complete. She was everything she needed to be, not the naïve, restricted girl in the picture. She and the person she admired most had bonded. And on top of that, she was happy with every aspect of her life.

It was a lovely spring day, and she wanted to enjoy every minute of it. First, she had to get some breakfast. Leaping up the stairs, she found Aisha sitting at the breakfast nook.

"You look happy," her landlady said, looking up from a stack of papers. "Is it because you got to see your friend?"

"Yes."

"So is this relationship going to change what's going on with you and my cousin? Patches is all man. Competing with an artistic enigma is not going to go over well."

Millie laughed, but it came out more like a snort. "No, the love I have for Taylar is different. I don't need Taylar here to know that we're connected. My relationship with Patrick is yet to be defined. By the way, how is your *friend?*"

Aisha put down her papers to look Millie in the eye, "To be honest, some things are better left alone. We have no business messing around with each other. But he won't go away, and I'm not sure I want him to leave. He saw Taylar yesterday, and from his reaction, I think they know each other. But he won't tell me how."

"And he probably will never tell you about his experience with Taylar. Knowing someone like Taylar can make a person greedy. You don't want to share. Like when you get your favorite dessert and don't want to share. Something happens in your brain from the moment it sees something desirable and procuring it. The anticipation of getting it. The effort that goes into the acquisition and finally tasting it. The sense of fulfillment and accomplishment. Round that up with the satisfaction of the moment being everything you thought it would be. Now, imagine all those feelings being tied to a person. It can feel like sensory overload. At least that is what it is like for me".

Aisha's jaw dropped, "So that means Taylar's a -"

"SHH!" Millie cut off her landlady quickly." None of us really knows, and we don't care. Taylar is Taylar."

Aisha dropped the subject and thought it would be better to adopt the Taylar fan club sentiment.

"Okay, moving right along, I forgot to tell you, Doris is pregnant. Also, I was kind of hoping you would renew our contract. Not that I need you to stay."

"Congratulations. And thanks, I've enjoyed living here. I can sign the forms when you're ready".

Aisha Raise "Here's to another year of living the exciting life."

www.ingramcontent.com/pod-product-compliance
Lightning Source LLC
La Vergne TN
LVHW091559060526
838200LV00036B/913